THE BELL STREET MURDERS

Borgo Press Books by S. Fowler Wright

Arresting Delia: An Inspector Cleveland Classic Crime Novel
The Attic Murder: An Inspector Combridge & Mr. Jellipot Classic Crime Novel
The Bell Street Murders: An Inspector Combridge & Mr. Jellipot Classic Crime Novel
Beyond the Rim: A Lost Race Fantasy
Black Widow: A Classic Crime Novel
The Capone Caper: Mr. Jellipot vs. the King of Crime: A Classic Crime Novel
Crime & Co.: An Inspector Cleveland Classic Crime Novel
Dawn: A Novel of Global Warming
Dead by Saturday: An Inspector Cleveland Classic Crime Novel
Dream; or, The Simian Maid: A Fantasy of Prehistory (Marguerite Cranleigh #1)
Elfwin: An Historical Novel
The End of the Mildew Gang: An Inspector Cauldron Classic Crime Novel (Mildew Gang #3)
Four Callers in Razor Street: An Inspector Combridge & Mr. Jellipot Classic Crime Novel
The Hanging of Constance Hillier: An Inspector Cleveland Classic Crime Novel
The Hidden Tribe: A Lost Race Fantasy
The Jordans Murder: An Inspector Combridge & Mr. Jellipot Classic Crime Novel
The King Against Anne Bickerton: A Classic Crime Novel
The Mildew Gang: An Inspector Cauldron Classic Crime Novel (Mildew Gang #1)
Murder in Bethnal Square: An Inspector Combridge & Mr. Jellipot Classic Crime Novel
The Police and the Public: Some Thoughts on the British System of Justice
Post-Mortem Evidence: An Inspector Combridge & Mr. Jellipot Classic Crime Novel
The Return of the Mildew Gang: An Inspector Cauldron Classic Crime Novel (Mildew Gang #2)
The Rissole Mystery: An Inspector Combridge & Mr. Jellipot Classic Crime Novel
The Screaming Lake: A Lost Race Fantasy
The Secret of the Screen: An Inspector Combridge & Mr. Jellipot Classic Crime Novel
Spiders' War: A Novel of the Far Future (Marguerite Cranleigh #3)
Three Witnesses: A Classic Crime Novel
Too Much for Mr. Jellipot: An Inspector Combridge & Mr. Jellipot Classic Crime Novel
The Vengeance of Gwa: A Fantasy of Prehistory (Marguerite Cranleigh #2)
Was Murder Done? A Classic Crime Novel
Who Murdered Reynard? A Classic Crime Novel
The Wills of Jane Kanwhistle: An Inspector Combridge & Mr. Jellipot Classic Crime Novel
With Cause Enough?: An Inspector Combridge & Mr. Jellipot Classic Crime Novel

THE BELL STREET MURDERS

An Inspector Combridge and
Mr. Jellipot Classic Crime Novel

by

S. Fowler Wright
Writing as "Sydney Fowler"

The Borgo Press

An Imprint of Wildside Press LLC

MMIX

CONTENTS

CHAPTER I.

You mean," Mr. Levinstein said, with no indication of his thoughts in a voice that came wheezily from his ample waistcoat, "that you eliminate the film entirely?"

The man to whom he spoke was seated at the far end of the boardroom table. He was shabby, and had the look of those whose hours of work are too long, and whose meals and sleep are too short. But he answered confidently, against the two rows of cold or sceptical eyes that were turned upon him.

"Yes, there's no need for a film. The surface takes it direct."

As he spoke the door opened. The last of the nine directors of Vantons, Ltd., a spare and active man with an air of cynical efficiency, entered the room, and took the chair which had been vacant at Mr. Levinstein's right.

That gentleman turned to him with a brief explanation of the business on which they were occupied.

"There's something here, Britleigh, on which we should like your opinion. It's one of those things that we get about twice a week that are going to revolutionize the motion-picture industry, and never do. But Groves thought it was worth having an option on it for three months.

"If it's a dud there's only a hundred gone, and if we take it there'll be a million to put up.... That's for a start, to buy the rights."

Lord Britleigh glanced down the table at the shabby applicant for a million pounds, sitting where so many had sat before with similar if somewhat more modest propositions, and from which so few had risen with satisfaction to themselves. If he knew him he gave no sign. He said carelessly, "We shall need half an hour before lunch on the Cunliffe contract. I've just seen Ward and Tucker.... But we'd better get this out of the way first. What's the idea?"

"Mr. Ralston had only partly explained it when you came in. It's an idea for eliminating the film, and using the screen direct."

I don't see any practical use in that, even possible. You'd need to make too many screens for each picture, and they'd be awkward things to send round. Worse than films, anyway.... Celluloid isn't that dear.... Besides...."

Groves thought that it might be worth while to hear what he's got to say."

Lord Britleigh signified an indifferent assent, and the Chairman wheezed again, in a somewhat higher key, to reach the lower end of the board.

"Lord Britleigh would like to know first: what are the commercial advantages that you claim for this invention? If you can't show a big saving in costs, it's no use bringing it here—not at that figure, anyway."

Mr. Ralston did not answer. He did not appear to hear. He was gazing at Lord Britleigh with expression of bewilderment, and with—was it hatred?—and appeared oblivious of surrounding circumstance.

"Mr. Ralston!" said the Chairman, in a more imperious wheeze. He was not used to being disregarded in this manner.

The inventor withdrew his eyes from the newcomer. He must have heard the Chairman's question, for he answered it without repetition, though in some confusion of words.

"If Mr. Warden…if Lord…. I'm afraid I can't answer that. I'm not a manufacturer. But if you don't take it up, I've no doubt someone else will. It's too big a thing to go begging far. If you don't take it, you'll have no costs at all."

"I don't think, Mr. Ralston," the Chairman answered, in his most important voice, "that I should rely too much upon it being a big thing. The big things are usually the most difficult to place. When you talk in millions there aren't more than three offices in London you can go into, if you go out of that door. Not that would listen to you, as we're listening now. Of course, we know that we should have no costs if we don't take it up. We don't need to be told that. We want to know just what you claim to do, and if it sounds worth our while we'll go into the question of whether you could hand over the goods."

"I didn't make myself quite clear," Mr. Ralston answered confidently. "I meant that if you don't take it up you'll have no costs at all. Not in the film industry anyway."

"We've heard that kind of talk before, Mr. Ralston. It cuts no ice with us. We've just listened, and sat tight, and we're still here. You'd better come to the facts."

Mr. Ralston had a strongly made leather attaché case before him. It was fastened with three locks. He drew three keys, one by one, from different pockets, and opened the case. He lifted from it a flat, heavy-seeming parcel wrapped in white paper.

"If I told you," he said, "you wouldn't believe. Nobody would. It'll save a lot of time if I show you this. I'm willing to pass it round the table, so that you can all see it in turn, but I want it quite dear that it will be returned to me before I leave the room. You'd better put that into writing, so that there'll be no mistake."

There was some delay over this, Mr. Levinstein considering that his word should be sufficient on such a point, and that, in any case, the terms of the option protected the inventor from any abuse of confidence. He said that they could not hope to do business if Mr. Ralston would not take his word "as among gentlemen" on such a matter.

But Mr. Ralston was firm. In the end, after some whispering at the upper end of the table, he had his way.

Mr. Ralston was told to write out the undertaking himself in any form he wished. The Chairman's manner indicated that the wording of such a document could be of no importance to the Board. They were simply humouring a man of a lower code than their own.

Showing no sign either of conceding the condition or resenting the manner in which it had been received, Mr. Ralston wrote out the required undertaking. The Chairman gave it an indifferent glance, and scrawled an illegible line beneath it which would have been good for half a million in the eyes of any banker in Europe. Ralston cut the string.

Mr. Sinfield, the secretary, seated at the Chairman's left, a man of a very orderly mind, seeing the careless use of the penknife, was led to wonder how the parcel would be reconstructed when the demonstration should be over.

Removing the paper, Mr. Ralston exposed an oblong slab of a smooth hard substance, opaque and pearl-white on its upper surface, and showing a dull slate-grey beneath as he lifted it clear.

He passed it to Mr. Nichols, the nearest of the directors, a man small and old, whose over-careful grooming could not disguise the aspect of one who had fought his way to affluence from the squalor of Limehouse. He looked at it with narrow, suspicious eyes as he turned it over, and would have passed it to his neighbour. His look was that of a man who cleared his hands of a clumsy attempt to defraud him.

"Wait a moment," interposed Mr. Ralston; "you haven't seen it yet." He reached forward to delay the passage of the stone.

He drew a small collapsible stereoscope from his pocket. Opening it, he inserted a duplicate view of such a scene as might be the commencement of any of a hundred of the masterpieces of Hollywood. It was a picture of sand and palms, with one of the principal kissers sitting half naked on a moonlit beach. "Please look through this," he said, "and fix your mind on the scene."

While Mr. Nichols did this, Mr. Ralston placed the stone uprightly behind the stereoscope. After a moment's pause he added, "Now please withdraw it, and look into the stone."

Mr. Nichols did so, but the scene at which he had been looking did not leave his eyes. He could see it now upon, or rather beneath, the surface of the stone. Only it had come to life. The palms moved in the wind. The tide rippled along the beach. The heroine began to skip about, as screen heroines do skip before kissing time has arrived.

Mr. Nichols was interested in what he saw. He was aroused by the voice of his left-hand neighbour. "After you, Nichols." He surrendered the stone with some reluctance. "It's a clever trick," he said sceptically. He looked at Mr. Ralston with more interest than before, wondering how it was done. He had no doubt that he was witnessing an attempt to "take in" the Board of Vantons, Ltd., which was naturally bound to fail; but he had more respect for Mr. Ralston as one of nerve and audacity to attempt it than he had had for him previously as a mere inventor.

But Mr. Ralston had at least succeeded to the point of having engaged the attention of the Board. The demonstration went on for nearly an hour before the last of the directors had had his turn. As one by one was added to the number of those who discussed what they had seen for themselves the animation grew. It became increasingly improbable that the Cunliffe contract would receive the half-hour of consideration which its importance required.

During this time Mr. Ralston sat silent. He said he would rather wait to answer questions till the demonstration had been concluded. With this the Chairman concurred. They could all give their attention then, and they would all know what they had to discuss.

Mr. Levinstein was silent also, except for an occasional word to deprecate discussion from others and a whispered query to Britleigh. "Who is the man...? Groves hadn't heard of him before. I saw that you knew him when you came in." But Lord Britleigh denied this. "He's a good deal like a man I once knew. A man who came to no good. A down-and-out now. But it isn't the same." He lied with a careless ease and a circumstanced invention which did not deceive Mr. Levinstein for a moment. Mr. Levinstein was not easily deceived, or he would not have been sitting where he was. He was quite sure of one thing, Mr. Ralston knew Lord Britleigh. He knew him under another name. He had called him Warden. Probably it was of no importance. But Mr. Levinstein did not forget.

"Well, gentlemen," he said, when the last of the directors had surrendered the stone and it was again in its owner's hands, "what do you make of it now?"

Mr. Nichols spoke first, repeating what he had said more than once previously. "It's no more than a clever trick."

"That's right enough, Nichols," said Mr. Ramsbottom, a man on the opposite side of the table, with a keen, lean face, who took pride in a reputation for being without imagination or sentiment, and being merciless in a business deal, "but it's the kind of trick that might pay. It's a clever trick, and we've paid a hundred quid to know how it's done, so we'd better hear."

Mr. Levinstein spoke again. "Gentlemen, the time's getting on. With your concurrence, I propose that Mr. Ralston should tell us briefly by what methods he produces this curious illusion in that stone, and what are the commercial possibilities which he claims for it. After that it may be most convenient for him to retire, and we will discuss whether it is a matter which we can entertain further."

Mr. Ralston replied that he could answer the first question very simply, the secret being entirely in the composition of the receiving surface, which could be easily and very cheaply made, and in any quantity. His difficulty was that he had not had the means to patent it throughout the world, which was an essential preliminary to its distribution. It seemed to him to be important, also, that it should be in the hands of those who would be financially strong enough to fight for the protection of their rights if it should be necessary to do so, for, he frankly admitted, if once the secret were known, its manufacture would be a very simple thing.

"It looks to me, gentlemen," said the Chairman, "as though it might be one of those things that are better handled as a secret process than as one that can be protected by the patent laws."

But Mr. Ralston was frank again in his assurance that that course would not be possible. "With this specimen in his laboratory, any chemist would give you its composition in a week—probably less than that. And so, gentlemen, with your permission...." he concluded, and, rising with the word, he walked over to the gate, in which a large fire burned—for it was the middle of January and the snow was three inches deep in the London streets—and dropped the slab into the glowing centre of the heat.

The dignity of the Board of Vantons, Ltd., did not prevent the common impulse that caused each director to twist round in his chair, or rise sufficiently to watch this unexpected conflagration. They saw that the slab burned quietly and easily, with a flame of cobalt blue, at which Professor Blinkwell, the technical adviser of the Board, looked with a particular interest. His eyes turned to Mr. Ralston. He seemed about to speak, and then checked himself, but the inventor answered the unspoken word. "Yes. That's it, of course. But it isn't all. That alone wouldn't take you far."

"No," said the Professor, with a friendly smile, "I don't suppose it would."

Mr. Nichols had been using a very quick brain at its top speed during the last few minutes. He had made a very difficult adjustment of his opinion of Mr. Ralston, or, at least, of the invention he offered. His mind was not impressed by the theatrical burning of the slab. It was too much like a conjurer's trick. Very clever some of those conjurers were. It would be a joke if it could be said that one of them had hoaxed the directors of Vantons. But in certain directions he had a respect for Professor Blinkwell's judgment. Not that the Professor was any good at business. Not the least. But he was firm on his own ground. He rarely made mistakes in the technical advice that he gave. The tone in which he had answered Mr. Ralston had not been such as he would have used to any conjuring clown.

"I hope," he said, "you've got that formula in a safe place."

"Yes, I think I have. Quite," Mr. Ralston smiled quietly, in an amused way.

"There aren't many safe places when a thing like that is concerned," Mr. Levinstein wheezed. "It ought to be in the strongest safe in the Chancery Lane vaults."

"It's better than that," the inventor answered. "It's in my own head."

"You mean," said Mr. Nichols, "it's a matter of memory? It's not written down at all? But suppose you were to die?"

Mr. Ralston was amused. "I'm afraid I couldn't carry on the negotiations if I did that."

"But our deposit…. It's not fair to us."

"I'm a fairly healthy man, but if you don't like the risk, it's a case for a quick deal."

"Gentlemen," the Chairman interposed, "we're not getting on as we should. We're a bit off the rails. We can take this point later, if we decide to go on with the thing at all. At present our second question has not been answered. We want to know: what are the commercial advantages that Mr. Ralston claims for this…this method of preparation? It doesn't go beyond that, as far as I can see."

"I think," the inventor answered quietly, "I'd rather leave you to judge of that for yourselves. You'll find it's got a good many points, if you think it out. But you'll judge what they're worth better than I. There's one thing I ought to tell you, though it's rather against myself. It requires a certain amount of concentration—not overmuch, but if the mind wanders it isn't always easy to pick up the picture. You might have to begin again.

The directors digested this information in a moment's silence, which Mr. Ramsbottom was the first to break. "Do you mean to tell us that this—whatever it is—could be used for a cinema? (He said "sinema," which is as usual in the film industry as in the East End of London.) The question was natural enough, but the tone and manner were those of a man who propounds that which his antagonist can only answer to his own confusion.

"Yes," said the inventor confidently. "Why not? Even at the stage to which I've developed it now—and it isn't likely to stop there—you'd only have to supply a stereoscope to each seat, with pictures of the opening scenes."

"And the first time a man turns his attention away he can't see any more?"

"I don't go that far. It's possible that the continuity would be broken."

"And then you think he'd sit there for a couple of hours, waiting for it to begin again? Well, he wouldn't. You can take that from me. It would be doomed at the start. They might come once, just to see a new thing. After that they'd keep away. If we'd wanted something to clear the cinemas right out you'd have brought us the goods."

There was a general murmur of assent at this verdict. The Chairman summed it up when he said, "We come back to this, Mr. Ralston. There'd be nothing in it when once the novelty had worn off. There's nothing from our point of view unless it shows a big saving in production costs, and even then it's no use if it wouldn't take on."

Mr. Ralston did not seem perturbed. He waited his time, and then said, "But there'd be no need for delay. If anyone wanted to start the picture again, he could do so at once."

Mr. Ramsbottom gave a thin-lipped smile of satisfaction. "I thought you'd say that. That's what shows the whole thing's a fake from end to end. You've forgotten that two men couldn't see different things on the same screen at the same time. How you do it I don't know; but anyone could see that. If you could start this at all, it would mean that everyone would have to think alike at the word 'Go,' and if they fell out of line because someone else came in late and trod on their toes, there'd be an end of the show for them. Not that anyone *would* come in late, because it wouldn't be any use if they did. The thing'd be no better than a washout, if it did all that you say. Mr. Chairman, I vote that we call it off, without wasting any more time."

"You may be right, Mr. Ramsbottom," the Chairman answered judicially, "but we'll hear what Mr. Ralston has to say."

That gentleman still seemed undisturbed as he answered, "But that is just what would happen. There is no reason why two people should not see different things on the screen at the same time. It's quite natural that they should. A mirror does just the same thing."

There was a confused murmur of protest at this statement. "A mirror only reflects what's there at the time."

"It only shows what's in front of it."

"It doesn't show two things at once."

Mr. Nichols, who had kept his mouth shut and his eyes on Blinkwell, was aware that the Professor looked interested. He didn't think he looked as though he thought the inventor were talking nonsense. Mr. Nichols didn't understand the illustration, but he saw that it was unlikely that Mr. Ralston would have made a statement which had no reason behind it. He didn't like Ramsbottom, and would be pleased to see him sat on by the rest of the Board. He asked at the first moment in which his voice could be heard, "What do you say to that, Professor?"

The question silenced the meeting to a recognition that the one of their number who was most competent to criticize had not yet been heard. He had the general attention when he answered. "There isn't an exact analogy, but Mr. Ralston's illustration is fair enough. If two men look at a mirror from different angles they will see different parts of the same scene depicted on the same surface of glass. The same part of the same surface will give different reflections at the same time to the two who look at it. I take it that Mr. Ralston means that there is nothing to prevent different members of an audience (though that is hardly the right word) from seeing different scenes on the same screen. It opens many possibilities."

Mr. Ramsbottom said he'd like Mr. Ralston to tell them how it was done.

"I can't tell you that, gentlemen. It's more than I know myself. I daresay it'll be simple enough when it's found out. But it's like electricity or ether—you can make use of them, and you know a lot about them, except only that you've no idea what they are! I've found out that a surface of this kind retains anything that is reflected upon it, though only in such a way that it can be seen by those whose eyes or minds are looking for what is there, but I can't go beyond that. It's no more than a photography in another form."

Professor Blinkwell asked, "What happens if you print a second picture on the same surface?"

"Yes," said the Chairman, "that's the real point. Apart from that...."

"As far as I know," Mr. Ralston answered, "you can print any number. The slab that I've just burnt had seventeen. I've made three before that, but I don't keep them longer than I need. That was the best of the lot. The difficulty's been to get the means of testing. The prints have not been easy to get."

"It's a great pity you burnt it as you did," the Chairman said seriously. "I don't see how we can settle anything till you replace it. We shall want to experiment a good deal beyond anything that we've done today."

But Mr. Ralston said that he would make no more, except on his own terms. He must have a contract to purchase. A definite binding agreement that the whole sum would be paid in a month, providing only that his invention fulfilled such tests as should be set out therein. When they had signed that he would make another of the mysterious slabs. He would give them the formula. It would be their risk if it were to become known before their patents were taken. He was not afraid that he could not fulfil the tests. If they signed such an agreement he knew that they would have to complete. But till then he would take no risks. It would remain concealed in his own mind. Anyway, he was sorry, but he must go now. He had an appointment for lunch. They could think it over, and write. Mr. Groves had his address. He got up to go.

Lord Britleigh spoke to the Chairman in a low voice. "We can't let him go like that. Do you think it would be any use if I had a word with him alone?"

The Chairman thought it would be a good thing to try.

Lord Britleigh followed Mr. Ralston out through the door. Mr. Ramsbottom remarked audibly as he saw him disappear that he shouldn't wonder if Britleigh meant to find out a bit for himself. Mr. Levinstein wheezed importantly that "Lord Britleigh has gone at my own request." He did not intend that Ramsbottom should think that he could rule *that* Board, be his place in the paper trade what it might.

Meanwhile Lord Britleigh had cornered Ralston in the waiting room below. He was saying, "Never mind about that. It's a good enough chance, and it wouldn't break us if it didn't prove all that you claim. Let me have her address, and you shall have the money within a week."

"I'll see you damned first," said Mr. Ralston, with the uncompromising directness of those who do not understand business.

"Oh. I wouldn't say that," Lord Britleigh answered lightly. "You might be damned yourself a bit sooner, if you don't alter your tone."

Mr. Ralston went without the courtesy of a parting word.

CHAPTER II.

RALSTON paused on the kerb. He had an appointment to meet Evelyn Merivale at one o'clock to lunch at Fletcher's restaurant, which is nearly opposite the offices of Vantons, Ltd. It was five minutes past now, and he knew that her time would be limited.

But he thought that he might be followed. He had not foreseen the possibility of meeting "Mr. Warden" in that boardroom, or he would have made a different appointment. He had no intention of being overreached in so absurdly simple a manner. After a moment's thought he lifted his hand to a passing taxi. He gave the man half a crown. "Drive along Oxford Street," he said, "toward the City. The first time you can turn round quickly into the opposite stream of traffic do so, and drop me at the kerb. You needn't go far."

It was an idea that had only occurred to him as he stood there, but he could see no flaw in it. It might be difficult for any following vehicle to imitate the unexpected turn in the crowded traffic. It would be impossible without making itself known. If it were not done immediately, the interval would be sufficient to enable him to disappear in the crowd. The last thing that would be expected would be his return to the street he had just left. We observe that Mr. Ralston had an alert and inventive mind.

Five minutes later he entered the first-floor dining-room at Fletcher's, and made his way to a table in one of the windows at which a girl was already seated.

"Evelyn," he said, in a low voice, without any precedent formality, "I've told the waiter we'll have another table."

The girl to whom he spoke gave him a smile of friendly recognition, showing neither resentment nor surprise at the abruptness of his address, but making no motion to comply.

"I don't think I'll move from here, Wilfrid. I like looking down into the street, and we're getting the sun, too."

"I've just seen Warden. He may be in the street now."

She looked down on a street from which there had not yet been time to clear the morning's snow-fall, but which was now bright with winter sunshine, and assured herself that the gentleman in question was not in sight. Then she rose without haste or loss of time, and moved over to the table that Mr. Ralston had chosen for her. She was almost of his own height, and of a figure which complied with the moment's demand for a universal slimness, though it may have done it with less than the average complacency. Simply dressed, she had the type of beauty which suggested the assurance of a gentle nurture. She had the air of one who would be self-possessed under any circumstances. She had a clearness of complexion and of grey eyes which appeared native to country lanes rather than to the dull pall of the London skies. She was not one who would pass unnoticed in any crowd. Her occupation was that of chauffeuse-secretary to Lady Barbara Dillington.

"Tell me," she said, when the meal was ordered and the waiter had retired to serve it, "how you have got on."

"Oh, they'll buy," he said. "They're a lousy lot, but they'll buy." He spoke without any tone of satisfaction at the fortune which was so near his hand. His mind was less upon that (which, after all, was no more than an expected thing since he had stumbled upon this discovery three months ago) than upon the meeting with the man whom he most wished to avoid.

But Evelyn Merivale appeared to be more interested in his financial negotiation. She said, "How much did you ask?"

"I put it at a million pounds; and I told Groves that I wouldn't come down sixpence, so they needn't waste time trying."

"Do you really think they'll pay that? It's a lot to ask."

"They can't help themselves. It's the biggest thing since the invention of wireless. They'll see that when they think it out. It means so many things. It means that people can go to a theatre and have the choice of a hundred films—or a thousand for that matter, as far as I can tell yet. Just as many as the opening pictures that are available for their inspection when they get to their seats. Probably there'll be a cabinet before each, with a proper index. If the theatres have records of the ones that are picked, they'll find out what people really like for the first time. And it's a curious thought that if the key-pictures should be lost there might be a hundred films buried in the screen that no one could ever see. There might be uncensored pictures that were only privately known…seditious pictures, or libellous…daring pictures of any kind that no one could prove to be there without the key-scenes to start them. There might be secret societies held together by such a link."

"It's a large sum, all the same."

"It won't be too much for you."

"It won't be mine at all, thank you. I'm quite content as I am."

"You promised you wouldn't…."

"Very well. We'll talk about something else."

Wilfrid Ralston looked at the girl with an anxious hunger, as a dog might look who is told to keep back from the plate of bones which has been put down for his expected meal. He could control his words more easily than he could keep this look from his eyes.

They were good friends, and she owed him something that she made no effort to forget, but she had held him off, all the same. while he had been poor. But a million pounds! He did not think that there could be many women in the world who would refuse that. Yet he aimed to win rather than to buy, bending all the subtlety of his mind to increase the intimacy of their relations and to win her regard.

He had a new thought. He would show his confidence, and establish another bond between them. He told her of the request that had been made for the formula, and of his reply that he trusted it to his memory only.

"It doesn't sound a very safe way," she said doubtfully. "Suppose you forgot."

"I shouldn't do that."

"Suppose something happened to you."

"You mean if I had an accident, or were taken ill? Well, I don't suppose I should be struck dumb, or have my right hand paralysed. Not both, anyway. If I did, I don't suppose the loss of the money would worry me afterwards. As a fact, I suppose I'm safer this way than any other. A man may be murdered who's known to carry a secret in his pocket worth a million pounds, but not if it's in his head. No, I wouldn't trust this to paper. I don't even trust Dudley with this."

"No," she said with decision, "I shouldn't trust Dudley."

"Still," he said, "I know that there's a risk that I ought not to take. I shouldn't like to think, if I did get knocked out, that you couldn't pick up the pile. There's no one looking at us behind, is there? I don't want to turn round."

"There's no one within hearing. There are two old ladies who have a good view of the back of your head, but they don't seem as interested as you might expect. There's a young girl facing us by herself not far away. She doesn't seem thrilled either. Still, she's doing her lips. She may hope that you'll look round. There's a man with his back to us three tables away."

Wilfrid Ralston did not respond to the lightness of her tone. He said seriously, "It sounds as though the ground's clear enough." He pulled out a small pocket-book and tore out a page, on which he wrote a few lines before passing it over to her. She looked at a column of five words and another of figures beside it.

She hesitated a moment, and then handed it back. "I'd really rather not have it," she said. "It's nice of you to trust me, but it's too great a responsibility. It might get lost."

"It wouldn't matter if it did. The two first lines mean nothing. They're put there to confuse. The other three have to be rearranged so that their initials will spell the word 'cub.' The figures must be left in the order they are, but with a one added to the left of each. Can you remember that?"

"Yes. That isn't hard. But I'd rather not. I'd much rather not have it at all."

"Well, I'd much rather you did. I should feel safer than I do now. I don't expect anything to happen, but I should like to know that it can still be pulled off if it does."

"But I shouldn't know what to do with the money. Wilfrid, have you any relatives besides Dudley?"

"My mother's living at Todmorden."

"Then give me her address, if you really want me to keep this. There's a man just come in who knows you. He's sitting down in the far corner on the left."

"What kind of man is he?"

"Small. Elderly. Well dressed. I don't want to be seen to look."

"Never mind. I shall know when I go out. Here's the address."

"You're giving me two."

"Yes, but don't notice that now. Can you drop one as you go out, so that this man will see it? It'll give him something to puzzle over, if he's up to no good."

"Very well, if you really wish. But it's rather silly, isn't it?"

"I can't tell, till I've seen who it is. There shouldn't be anyone who knows me coming in here. But never mind him. I want to talk to you about Warden. The question is: can he find you through the address I've given Groves?"

"I don't see why he should. They think it's yours, and you've told them only to write. But you haven't told me yet where you saw him, or how."

"He's one of Vantons' directors. He followed me out, and offered to get the deal through in a week if I'd give him your address."

Evelyn received this information, as her way was, without giving any sign of her thought to the jealous watchfulness of his eyes. She said:

"That does make it rather a risk, but I don't see what I can do. I can't tell all the servants that they're to say I don't exist if Lord Britleigh calls."

"Lord Britleigh? I didn't mention that name. Then you knew...."

If she had made a slip, she allowed no confusion to appear as she answered: "Yes, I knew that."

He was suddenly aware of the lack of any real intimacy between them: of the extent of ground which he had to gain before he could hope to succeed in the purpose that was always in his mind. But he was too adroit to force a discordant issue.

He said, "Well, I suppose we'll have to go now. It might be best to keep together till we know we're not followed. But I don't mean to go back to Hoxton tonight. If anyone's following me they'll cover some ground in the next two days. You can readdress any letters to Twickenham as usual. Don't look at the man as you go out, but drop it where he'll be sure to see it after you've passed."

CHAPTER III.

It was a mere chance that had brought Mr. Nichols to that corner table. Fletcher's restaurant, though comfortable enough, is not usually patronized by the magnates of Vantons, Ltd. But the board-meeting had been prolonged, and Mr. Nichols was short of time for a private interview which he had arranged for the afternoon. The varied experiences of his sixty-one years had left him about equally at home in a palace or a fried-fish shop. He came to the nearest place that could give him the food he needed. He was not concerned, nor greatly interested, when he observed that Mr. Ralston was also patronizing the establishment with a lady friend. Yet the bodily presence of the inventor may have contributed to hold his mind to the subject of the morning's interview. He had already decided that if it were not nothing at all (as most new things turned out to be) it was a very big thing indeed. It did not follow that they should pay the price which was asked. A million is a large sum. He always thought that Mr. Levinstein was too easy in those ways, as were most of his co-directors. They either refused a thing entirely, or they looked for their profit by making a big deal, rather than by haggling with the vendor. Keen though they were, they thought of large sums in an easy way. But he had been brought up in a penurious school. For many years the only money he made had been that which he didn't spend. He had often interposed successfully to reduce the amount at which they would purchase an idea or an interest. "Now it's your turn, Nichols," his co-directors would say when they had passed a resolution to purchase. He was accustomed to study those with whom they had dealings, to judge how best they could be handled at the moment when the principle is agreed and amounts and details have to be settled.

He met Mr. Ralston's eyes as the two passed his table, and gave him a friendly nod of recognition, which Ralston, in his own way as keen and subtle as himself, rightly judged to indicate that the Board had passed a favourable resolution after he left it. He looked at Evelyn with appraising and approving eyes. He saw the paper on the floor after she had passed. He did not see it fall, for it had been dropped from her farther side. But he knew it had not been there a moment before. As they went out of sight, down the turn of the stairs, he reached to retrieve it.

It had not occurred to him to call Evelyn's attention to it. Unless he had aimed to make her acquaintance, what object could there have been? He looked at it carelessly, not expecting anything of importance or interest.

He read an address—37 *Willow Rd., East Ham*. That was all. It was a man's handwriting. Probably Ralston's. He could easily verify that. Presumably one that he had just given her. Why should he give her an address of such a character? In the East End of London. As to that he could only speculate. But when a man is in control of an invention which he values at a million pounds everything he does is of interest. This might be the secret factory where the material was made. Even the formula might be there. He had said that he carried it only in his own mind, but that might not be true. He had admitted that anyone who had a piece of the material had the secret in his own hand. A million pounds is a large sum to save. As he considered that point the probability that he held the address of the secret factory asserted itself more plausibly. Might not the woman be one whom Ralston had just engaged, perhaps as secretary, and so he had given her his address? It would be like his caution to interview her first at such a place. Well, if that were so, it seemed unlikely that she would keep her next morning's appointment.

When he got back he looked in at the General Manager's office. "By the way, Groves," he said, "what address did Ralston give you?"

"We write to him at 13 Belleville Gardens, S.W.3. He asked us to communicate only by letter."

"Accommodation address? It hardly sounds like it."

"No. I had it looked up, of course. Lady Barbara Dillington lives there."

"What sort's she?"

"Oh, excellent reputation. Wealthy. Dull. Sixty-eight. Cousin to Lord Chislehurst."

"Queer," said Mr. Nichols thoughtfully. "He wouldn't have his workshop there. I suppose he isn't one of the servants. He hardly looks the part. I wonder whether we've got his right name. By the way, Groves, I suppose you've had the resolution down from the boardroom? Well, don't send the letter for a couple of days. We might do better. Anyway, it'll do no harm to keep him in suspense for a day or two. And find out for me who lives at 37 Willow Road, East Ham. Let me have a private report about that. Put someone on it at once."

This was ten days before the London evening papers were able to sell an extra fifty thousand copies by the announcement of the Hoxton murder.

CHAPTER IV.

HOXTON, which was once a rural hamlet a few miles from London, is now one of its foulest and most congested areas. In summer it has sunless heat and dust, and its babies die; in winter it has sunless cold and rain, and its older people perish. Seldom does the heavy gloom of its dirt-encumbered air lift sufficiently to expose it to a ghostly mockery of sunshine. Never, for a generation, has it known a summer sky of clean white cloud and bare un-blinded blue.

Yet here, where it might seem that mankind had sought to create a forecast of their waiting hell, where it might be thought that life would dwindle, shrinking from reluctant birth, it rises fecund and defiant. It holds its own in hell, and goes forth. After counting its tale of death, disease, and deformity, it has still a surplus of gallant youth, hardened by privation, that will carry their Cockney courage and their Cockney humour into many cities and seas. It is amid the luxury of London's western side that life dwindles and shrinks, proving the hardest lesson of life—that even disastrous battle is better than enduring peace. It is there that we must look for the futile childless women, the timid men who hesitate and hoard and fear.

The pavements of River Street are never quiet, being littered with children, and loud with the voices of women who nurse their babies on the steps of their open doors; but it has little of pedestrian traffic, though there is a constant rattle of heavy lorries that turn aside from the narrow congestion of St. John's Road, preferring a somewhat longer way by which they can make better speed, with no risk of anything more important than the lives of the children who dodge and sometimes die beneath their indifferent wheels. Most of its length River Street shows no variation in the rows of its smoke-blackened houses, the doors of which open on to the pavement, less than twelve feet apart. But at the farther end on the south side (before you reach the canal) there is the blank wall of an old factory, which has been unoccupied since the end of the post-War boom, and which Messrs Shard and Nesbitt offer vainly either to lease or sell. Between this derelict building and the nearest house there is a narrow unlighted entry which bends slightly after the first three or four yards, so that its upper end is out of sight of the street. Sometimes at night there may be shadows that slip into it for some murky purpose, but in the daytime it has the isolation that is possible in congested areas to unregarded familiar things. Only some occasional stranger may enter it in the mistaken hope that it will provide him with a short cut to Bell Street, and will turn back from a final obstacle of unwindowed wall, and with little interest in the dirty door that is closed at his left-hand side.

This door is of no great strength, and anyone examining it on January 13, 1930, would have observed nothing unusual except that it had a large and recent keyhole in addition to the higher one which was of the ordinary latch-key size. But it may be doubted whether anyone had seen this keyhole since it had been made, about two months earlier, or had come so far up the passage in daylight hours, unless it were those who made use of the door, and they themselves might have been observed to be of somewhat nocturnal habits, had it been anyone's business to regard their movements.

It was about three hours after sunset when Mr. Dudley Ralston came up the entry. He showed his familiarity by the pace at which he moved in the narrow darkness, and by the ease with which he inserted the heavy key which he had already drawn from his hip-pocket. The latch-key followed. The door opened into an unlighted interior, and was quickly closed. There was the sound of the turning of the lock, another sound as of the dropping of a heavy bar; and then silence, until a man moved from the blackness of the passage-end, not two yards away.

He cast a torch-light casually over the closed door, and with more deliberation over the space of the wall which had divided him from the man whose key had been in the lock. He bent as though he were himself turning such a key. He stood at the wall again, and reached out with his arm toward the door, keeping the light upon it. When he had satisfied himself in these particulars he extinguished the torch and went away.

Meanwhile Mr. Dudley Ralston had switched on a light which revealed a narrow length of hall, with uncarpeted wooden stairs at its farther end. Passing up these stairs, he came to a bare landing from which he entered a living-room that was plainly though untidily furnished, and of sufficient comfort for one who was satisfied with the essentials of warmth and food. He lit a gas-fire in the grate, and drew closer the heavy curtains, though it was improbable that there could be any to observe him, for the window opened to an interior yard of the abandoned factory. He spread an old newspaper on the table, and fetched some crockery and tinned food—biscuits and pilchards—from a cupboard. It might be judged that he did not live regularly in this cheerless house, but that the food was there against a casual emergency.

Having commenced the meal, he looked at his watch, as though expecting an interruption that did not come.

Finishing it, he went out on the landing, crossing it by the light of the door that he had left open behind him. He paused at the opposite door, striking a match, and observing that a narrow thread which he had stretched across it was still unbroken. Judging thereby that his brother had not been there in his absence, he turned away without troubling to use the illicit key which his pocket held. He had searched the secrets of that room so thoroughly before he had stretched that thread. If there had been a line of writing which could have given him the guarded secret, a piece of the strange substance, though it were but of a crumb's size. But it was useless to search again till Wilfrid had been.

As he came back to the lighted room a telephone-bell rang. He went quickly to an instrument on the wall, and took off the receiver. "That you, Myra? Yes, I got your message. I've been here half an hour, came straight without waiting to get any dinner, and had to pig it as best I could. No, I can't say I have. It's easy to say that, but it isn't easy to do. Anyway, I'm through now. Yes, *through.* Well, that's plain enough, isn't it? Yes, you can tell the Chief. I don't care either way, but it's safer than for us to meet again. Tell him…. Well, I'm not, anyway. Tell him to go to hell. Of course not, why should I?

He rang off, hearing his brother's step on the stairs.

CHAPTER V.

THE TWO brothers met civilly, but without cordiality. Seen together, they were of an obvious similarity, but Dudley, about three years the younger, had a more self-indulgent aspect. He was better dressed; he looked better fed. His face had signs of dissipation from which his brother's was free. The inventive subtleties of Wilfrid's mind appeared in Dudley to be duplicated by cunnings of a more animal and, perhaps, of a more predatory kind.

"Any letters for me?" Wilfrid asked.

"I haven't looked. I asked you not to have any sent here. It isn't safe."

"Well, you know I never have. I've only given the address in one direction, as a last resort. But I've been two days at Twickenham, expecting a very important one that hasn't come."

"Then you haven't sold?"

"Wait a moment. I'll just see if there is."

He went down and struck a match in the darkness of the front hall. Its door opened to Bell Street, or would have done so had it ever been opened at all. It was a door of no great strength, and so ill-fitting that there was a visible space between it and the step which descended to the street level, and its rusty lock and two bolts would have given way quickly enough to an active assault, but what was there to tempt it in the dust of the empty hall, as it could be seen through the slit which had been cut for a letter-box which was no longer there? The postman, if he thought of it at all, must have regarded it as having been unoccupied for the last two years, but that would not alter his duty to deliver any letter which might be clearly addressed to No. 30.

But there was no letter in the hall.

"Something gone wrong?" Dudley inquired, observing his brother's empty hands and irritated expression as he re-entered the room.

"No. I don't suppose so. Only an annoying delay."

"You should have let me handle it for you. I bet you'll make a mess of it somehow. I'd have got double your price, anyway."

"How much would you have asked?"

"You can't expect me to say that, offhand. You have to feel your way in such deals. If you'd shared with me, or even given me a decent commission, I daresay I'd have got fifty thousand, if it does all that you say."

"You've seen that for yourself."

"Yes, I know. But it doesn't seem a possible thing. It seems as though it might be a trick, somehow."

"Well, it's a trick that works. What commission should you have thought fair?"

"Well, anyone gets ten percent, and there's you having had the room—"

"I've paid you for that."

"—and all the test, and we being brothers. You couldn't have made it less than twenty."

"Twenty percent, and you'd have tried for fifty thousand? You'd have made ten thousand out of that."

"Yes, and not a penny too much."

"I didn't say that it was. I've always told you that I'd give you a share if I pulled it off. If I do, I'll give you the ten thousand."

"You must be asking a lot."

"I'm asking a million pounds."

Dudley stared at his brother. Even his audacity wouldn't have tried anything like that. He made a rapid calculation. Ten thousand was one percent…a miserable return for the accommodation he had given. And he had already said that he would throw up his present occupation in the assurance of *this*. He did not reflect that ten thousand pounds was the utmost hope that he had had previously on the result of his brother's promise. It was the difference in the percentage that made the sum contemptible which had seemed so large a few minutes earlier. His brother a millionaire, and him with—ten thousand pounds! He said, "You can't really mean that you think one percent's a fair deal. I shouldn't treat you like that."

"No," his brother answered dryly, "I didn't say that you would. It isn't a fair deal at all. It's a free gift."

"I don't see that, even if we weren't what we are. You've had the use of this place, and there isn't anywhere where you'd have been quieter, or less likely to get overlooked. It's been a godsend to you, and I told you from the first that it's doing a lot to let you come here. I don't want anything to draw attention to this address."

"Well, nor do I; and so far nothing has. We both wanted the same thing; and every week I've paid you the rent you asked, whether it's been easy or not, and I haven't wanted to know what you are doing here. I don't see what it matters to you what I've done either."

"That's how you talk now you think you've pulled it off. When you said I should have a share if it came out right I didn't think you meant a miserable one percent, and I don't think you did either. And I'm not even sure of that. I've got nothing in black and white. If you'll just give me a line that you'll pay me the ten thousand, I'll take it for what it's worth, and hope you won't really be so mean when you've picked up the cash."

"I shan't give you a line, and I'll take back what I said if you haven't got the sense to shut up. It's a mere gift;

and, anyway, I haven't got the cash yet, and we don't know that I ever shall. There ought to have been a letter for me before this. Well, it's no use staying now."

Wilfrid went at this, his brother following him to the stairhead to call, "I suppose you'll be coming back, but I mayn't be here much after today. You'll always be able to get me at East Grinstead. You'll let me know how you get on?"

He had an uneasy feeling that he hadn't managed the conversation very successfully. Thinking it over, he decided that he would be there a good deal, if not for his old purpose. Wilfrid would be back to continue his experiments, to manufacture more of the secret material, he had no doubt of that. And he would be there also, at other times, and with the bolt on the back door, so that Wilfrid could not disturb him at the wrong moment. If the secret were once in his hands....

CHAPTER VI.

LADY BARBARA DILLINGTON had been accustomed to rule her household with a firm though kindly discipline. For many years she had exercised a supervision over its correspondence which would be resented by a modern servant. She had held the sole key of the letterbox, and its contents had been distributed by her own hands, and not always without some inquiries as to the nature of the letters which she handed to those for whom they were addressed. With advancing years and consciousness of other changes, she had abandoned this habit, or rather modified it to the extent of providing her secretary with a duplicate key, and leaving the routine distribution of the contents of the box in her capable hands.

It followed that when Mr. Ralston had confided to that young lady that he wished for an address from which he could correspond securely, she had told him that any communication addressed to 13 Belleville Gardens would come first under her own eyes, and could be forwarded to him. At the worst (and very remote) possibility of Lady Barbara opening the box, such a letter could only be returned to the post-office as one that had been addressed in error—and, almost certainly, this duty would be allotted to her, and she would be able to deal with it at her own discretion.

So far this method had worked with its expected smoothness. The preliminary correspondence with Vantons, Ltd., had been so conducted that they would have found it very difficult to spy upon Mr. Ralston's activities had they attempted to do so, and that gentleman had achieved a further and equally important object in establishing a reason for communicating with Miss Merivale, and securing her interest in the negotiation in which he was occupied.

It was on the third morning after the directors' meeting which he had attended that Mr. Groves approached Mr. Nichols with a query as to whether he should further delay the letter which the Board had instructed him to issue.

"Mr. Levinstein's been asking me whether I'd got a reply, and he seemed rather annoyed when I said you'd asked me to hold it back."

"That's all right, Groves. That's not your funeral. What have you found out about that address at East Ham?"

"I've got this report, sir. It seems to cover the ground." He handed Mr. Nichols a typewritten document.

> The address given has been occupied for over ten years by Mr. Jacob Withers, an antique-dealer. He is a man of about sixty-five, living with an unmarried daughter, Miss Josephine Withers. They live very quietly, having no servants, and very few callers. Mr. Withers has a shop at 217 Gray's Inn Road, which he attends daily. The rent of 37 Willows Road is 14s. weekly. It is always regularly paid. The local tradespeople give Mr. Withers a good character. He spends little, but runs up no accounts. There appears to be no gossip about either himself or his daughter. Most of the adjacent houses are occupied by dock labourers or artisans, and it does not appear that Mr. or Miss Withers are on familiar terms with any of them.

Mr. Nichols considered this information. It was evident that his first surmise had been inaccurate. He now concluded that this was an address which Mr. Ralston had recommended to a new employee as a suitable place at which she might lodge. Having lost the address, she had probably not availed herself of the recommendation. Therefore, it could give no due either to his address or hers, beyond the probability that it was near the site of Mr. Ralston's mysterious experiments. Still, he was presumably known to the antique-dealer. That might be worth following up. For the moment his mind returned to the address which they had received in a more legitimate way— that of Lady Barbara Dillington—the address which he had given as his, and which almost certainly wasn't.

"Groves," he said, "you can send the letter. Send it registered, and ask the post-office to supply a certificate of delivery."

CHAPTER VII.

MR NICHOLS was annoyed. He had called upon Miss Josephine Withers, as a single gentleman seeking rooms, and had been sourly received. Miss Withers had informed him in the course of a doorstep interview that she did not let rooms, never had let rooms, never meant to let rooms, and did not believe that anyone had ever said that she did. She did not know anyone of the name of Wilfrid Ralston, nor of William Sykes, nor of Charles Peace, but she knew Bill Picktub next door, who would come at once if she knocked twice on the wall, and could choke Mr. Nichols with the thumb and finger of one hand. If he waited till she called the police he would be a sillier man than she thought he was. Mr. Nichols went.

It was on the following morning that he recounted his experience to Professor Blinkwell. He did not hesitate to narrate the way in which the address had come into his hands. Everyone recognized that though the Professor was not a business man, and did not appreciate the ethical standards which prevail in the circles of successful commerce, yet he was tolerant in judgment upon the acts of his friends.

"There's something very queer," Mr. Nichols concluded, "about that Ralston, whether his invention's a fake or a fortune, and I'm not oversure about that. I saw him write that address and give it to the young woman who dropped it as she went out, and why on earth should he have done that if he didn't know the people who lived in the house? It isn't sense. And if she knew him, why did she give me her tongue as she did?"

The Professor was mildly sympathetic, perhaps mildly amused. He said casually, when Mr. Nichols was about to pass on to his own office, "I can give you his address, if you really want it. I don't mean Belleville Gardens. I mean where he works."

Mr. Nichols looked his surprise. "How on earth—" he began.

"Quite simply," said the Professor. "I didn't pick anything up. I just wrote and asked."

So in fact it had been. The device of the registered-letter certificate which had occurred to the ingenuity of Mr. Nichols having somewhat overreached itself, as such cleverness is apt to do, had some indirect bearing upon this development.

Had the postman asked for no more than the signature which is required on delivery of every registered packet, it is probable that the butler would have given it without a too-curious examination of the letter to which it related, but being asked to put his name to a less familiar document, he was led to a more critical consideration, and while he was debating with the postman his ignorance of Mr. Ralston's name, it chanced that Lady Barbara descended the stairs. Two minutes later the postman went down the steps with the registered letter in his bag.

The next morning Miss Merivale, opening the letter-box as usual, found an unregistered envelope for Mr. Ralston, and readdressed it to Twickenham. Mr. Ralston received it at a time when he was becoming anxious at the continued silence of the Board. It read thus:

DEAR MR RALSTON,

I have been thinking over your invention with much interest. If you would grant me the privilege of meeting you in your own laboratory, as a brother scientist, I should account it an honour, and should be glad to talk over some of the possibilities which your invention appears to offer.

Yours sincerely,

ELIHU BLINKWELL

Mr. Ralston sat for half an hour in Richmond Park, in the faint warmth of a wintry sunshine, reflecting upon this letter. He did not intend to incur any risk of communicating his secret to the Professor, or anyone else, till he had got his agreement signed in the form in which he had asked for it to be. But he was confident that he could avoid any such risk. The formula was buried in his own brain, from which it would be difficult for anyone to abstract it without his consent. He misread the delay which had occurred in the receipt of any communication from the Board. He concluded that they had probably failed to arrive at a united decision. This overture from the Professor might be of a decisive importance. If he could satisfy him—which was sufficiently probable—it might be that it would be the means of turning the scale in his favour. He went back, and wrote:

13 BELLEVILLE GARDENS, S.W.3
January 16th, 1930

DEAR PROFESSOR BLINKWELL,

For reasons which you will readily understand, I have not previously invited anyone to my laboratory, the address of which I have kept strictly private during the progress of my experiments.

Your position is, however, exceptional, both in respect of your personal attainments, and as a director of the firm with whom I am negotiating.

If you can come tomorrow (Friday) evening conveniently, arriving at Old Street Station at about 8:30 P.M., I will meet you there, as our destination—which would not be very easy to find by written directions—is quite near. In that event there will be no necessity to answer this letter.

Yours sincerely,

WILFRID RALSTON

The Professor had kept the appointment, and had accompanied Mr. Ralston along the narrow streets, and followed him up the unlighted passage, and through the silence of the half-furnished house, without hesitation or undue curiosity. On being seated in the laboratory, he had relieved Mr. Ralston's mind at once by handing him the returned registered packet, and, with an habitual courtesy which might not have occurred to his more commercial-minded colleagues, he had relieved him of any necessity for explanation by suggesting that their manager had made an error of judgment in requiring the post-office to obtain a certificate of delivery, "which would naturally be unobtainable if you should have been absent when it was tendered."

Opening it, Mr. Ralston read that the Board had decided to accept his offer. They had given instructions for a draft agreement to be prepared, by which he would undertake to supply them forthwith with the secret formula, for which they would pay him the sum of one million pounds within one calendar month of that date, provided only that he had demonstrated during that time that his invention fulfilled the conditions set out in the original option. They invited him to meet the Board at 11 A.M. on Friday, the 24th instant, when the agreement would be in readiness, and could be signed immediately if it should have his approval. Mr. Ralston's solicitor would be present, should he desire to be legally advised on that occasion.

Mr. Ralston had been naturally pleased. He may have been more than usually expansive under the influence of this communication, and with the stimulus of the Professor's conversation, but he lost neither his head nor his formula, nor, to be just to the Professor, did he attempt to take any unfair advantage of him.

"He'll be here," the Professor now continued to Mr. Nichols, "for the board meeting next Friday, but if you like to see him beforehand, you can write and ask. Say I suggested it, if you like. It might help a bit. I think we got on fairly well."

"Coming Friday, is he? Then he's had the letter. I don't see that I can do much after that. I daresay I could have saved about £900,000 if they'd left it to me. Perhaps more. But I'll try to see him, all the same. There's something damned queer about that man, and it mayn't be any loss to us to find out what it is."

"I can't say I saw anything queer," the Professor answered. "I thought him a very intelligent man."

Mr. Nichols agreed to his intelligence. He added, "I don't think I shall write. I shall just pay him an unexpected call. There'll be no gain for him to think things over before we meet."

The Professor looked doubtful about that. The address had been given to him in a somewhat confidential way. Still, if Mr. Nichols felt sure. He went on to give such directions for the finding of the River Street entry as appeared to show that if he were deficient in commercial acumen he had other mental powers which were by no means contemptible.

CHAPTER VIII.

IT was on Monday afternoon, the 20th, that Mr. Nichols obtained Mr. Ralston's address from the Professor. The following morning he took a taxi to River Street. He paid off the driver with his accustomed parsimony, but told him that he should probably not be many minutes and he could wait if he liked, and drive him back. But it was his risk; it might be longer. He went up the entry to a locked door, knocked and knocked again without response, and concluded reasonably that Mr. Ralston was not there.

He was about to turn away when Mr. Dudley came up the passage. He looked at his unexpected caller with a curiosity which was without friendliness. It was clear that their destination was the same door. There was no choice. Mr. Dudley made no assault upon the door. It might be assumed that he had his own means of access. Mr. Nichols stood his ground. Mr. Dudley made no motion to knock while he was there. He was the first to speak. "Are you looking for anyone?"

"I want to see Mr. Wilfrid Ralston."

Mr. Dudley looked annoyed, and felt more so. He did not welcome visitors of any kind. Particularly such as he did not know. Particularly such as left taxis standing in the street. The man might be any kind of spy. But it might be an error of tactics to make mystery of a simple thing. He said, "I don't suppose he's about here. Could I tell him who is inquiring, if I happen to run across him?" That was vague enough. It gave nothing away, unless he should have denied that he knew who his brother was.

Mr. Nichols drew out a card. Mr. Dudley read it, and his manner changed. On his side he drew out a key. He said, "Perhaps you'd like to wait inside. He might be here any time. I couldn't ask you in till I knew who you were. He's very particular about keeping his experiments quiet." He thought it a neat touch to attribute his previous attitude to his brother's scruple. Mr. Nichols followed him into the house.

It was an hour later when he came out, and there was no lack of geniality on the part of the man who parted with him at the door. They had understood each other very quickly, and very well. If Mr. Dudley could steal the secret of his brother's invention before Friday next, it would be worth not £10,000, but £50,000—a much more considerable and satisfactory figure. Mr. Nichols would come again on Wednesday night—late. Mr. Dudley did not mind how late. It would be the more certain that Mr. Wilfrid Ralston would not be there. Very well. Twelve o'clock. Midnight. That would do.

CHAPTER IX.

MISS EVELYN MERIVALE was in excellent spirits. She had had an exceptionally good lunch at the Savoy. She had refused a proposal of marriage, which is an enjoyable experience when you are sufficiently sure that it will be repeated, and although (she told herself) she had not the slightest intention of marrying Wilfrid Ralston, though he should become a millionaire a dozen times, yet she was conscious of a pleasant excitement at the magnitude of the approaching transaction, and in the assurance of triumph which had induced the midday expenditure of three pounds seven shillings upon a quantity of food which could have been procured for six-and-three pence without any great difficulty, and at a time when he had mentioned that his bank account contained a credit of seven pounds.

She had taken Lady Barbara out during the afternoon for some shopping in Oxford Street (Lady Barbara, with Victorian frugality, though unable to spend more than about a tenth of her income, always took full advantage of the reductions of the January sales), and was walking back through the wet street from the Calthorpe Garage, when she became aware that another forward step would bring her into collision with Lord Britleigh, whose position was supported on the one side by a rather fat woman, and on the other by the area railings. Declining the vulgar expedient of a collision which might not have removed the obstacle, or the ignominious one of a strategic movement to the rear, she stood still before a man who neither raised his hat nor offered his hand, and who lacked the excuse of surprise for these familiar discourtesies.

"Well, Evelyn," he said, "so here we are."

Miss Merivale was a young lady of self-possession and self-control, and though the meeting was abrupt, she had foreseen its possibility. The fat woman had passed on, and Evelyn continued in the same orbit. "Still making piles, I suppose," she remarked pleasantly to the man, who had turned, and was now walking beside her. Lord Britleigh did not respond to this gambit. He noticed her quickened step, and said querulously, "Look here, Evelyn, I want a talk. I haven't seen you for nearly a year, and there are things that you ought to know. I haven't even been able to send you the parrot that old Mrs. Quinney left you when she died, and I hate the sight of the bird. I always hated it when we used to go there when we were kids."

We may observe the adroitness of Lord Britleigh, who certainly had not sought Miss Merivale to discuss parrots, but who knew the importance at certain stages of conversation of introducing matter of interest to the other side.

"Is the old dame dead? I'm sorry about that. Not that you care a straw. Or about the parrot either. You know, Cyril, you're very like Wilfrid in some ways."

"Wilfrid...? Oh, you mean that...."

"Yes, of course. You don't suppose I call him Mr. Ralston, do you? Cyril, you're showing your age more than you need. You're Pre-war."

"You've not gone and engaged yourself to that...."

"Inventor. You don't love him, do you? He doesn't love you overmuch. Not any more since he learnt your real name, either."

"I suppose you think he'll be a millionaire in a month. Well, I came to give you a straight tip not to be too sure. You couldn't *want* to marry a bounder like that, and I don't want you to give your word, and then not know how to back out. I'll tell you this straight, the deal wouldn't go through, even now, if I drew out. They couldn't do without my share of the cash. Not easily, anyway. And Ramsbottom'd follow me, and one or two others besides. Well, I want your word that you're not engaged to him, and don't mean to be, or...."

"You needn't go on saying all the dirty things that you're ready to do, because I told him about an hour ago that I'm no more likely to marry him than to marry you. Cyril, suppose you tell me who *could* marry—with one exception, of course—without you trying to make mischief about it. So if you don't let the deal go through, you'll only damage yourself and your friends, and for no purpose at all. I'm going to walk once round the square with you before I go in, and if you've any news to give me of how things are at Saxton, I shall be glad to hear, so long as you keep off one subject which we both know, and if you start on that I shall walk straight in. And after that I want you to promise not to come here again. Lady Barbara'd want to know more about you than I could easily tell."

"I don't know what there is to tell you particularly, if you won't be sensible and come home. Of course, I take your word. But I shouldn't be too sure of him pulling it off, all the same. There's something queer about the whole matter, and we're not the board to leave anything to chance in a deal of this size. Levinstein's got Blinkwell and Nichols working on it now." He stopped, as though conscious of a possible indiscretion, and Miss Merivale became aware at the same moment that they were at the gate of No. 13, but she did not call attention to that circumstance. Rather, her attitude thawed to an increased friendliness as she commenced a second perambulation. She began to talk about the invention, its nature and prospects, as she had gathered from Mr. Ralston's explanations. She was too adroit to give a direct opening for Lord Britleigh to guess her purpose, and between her own cau-

THE BELL STREET MURDERS, BY S. FOWLER WRIGHT

tion of approach and his natural reticence on such a position she learnt little beyond one specific fact, the significance of which she could appreciate in the light of what she had learnt at her lunchtime conversation. Mr. Nichols was going to—Lord Britleigh did not say, perhaps did not know, where—but *somewhere* that night, from which *something*—he did not say, perhaps did not know, what—inimical to Wilfrid Ralston's interests was likely to follow. Possibly Lord Britleigh was as alert as Miss Merivale to the purpose with which she developed the conversation. He made it clear that she could have his help very fully to any purpose she would if she would return to her own home with the implications that such an action would bear. He may have aimed to say no more than would vaguely alarm her as to the plots which were proceeding. They were both of the conversational habit which uses understatement rather than emphasis. If a vague hint of danger to Mr. Ralston's fortunes left her unmoved, it would indicate that her interest in him was really of a moderate kind, which was what Lord Britleigh was most anxious to know. Considered as a contest of wits, it may have been no more than a drawn battle. But its after-consequences were of a different pattern. It left certain facts and one inference clear in Miss Merivale's mind. Mr. Nichols was going *somewhere* tonight. Mr. Nichols and Professor Blinkwell had been mentioned as working together in hostility to Mr. Ralston. Professor Blinkwell had already penetrated to the River Street laboratory. Doubtless Mr. Nichols would be proceeding in the same direction. She knew that Wilfrid was intending to spend the night there upon some final preparations for his next demonstration. She was certain that he was not expecting such a visitor. She knew that he was suspicious of Dudley, of whom she knew enough to distrust him thoroughly. She felt vaguely that there was a danger of which Wilfrid should be warned. Because she did not contemplate marriage, it did not follow that the claims of friendship were silent. She had been in Wilfrid's confidence from the first. She had helped him by receiving and redirecting the correspondence. She had a natural interest in the spectacular success of that with which she had been associated. Besides, she was of a natural loyalty in her friendships. And his frequent proposals of marriage must not be overlooked. At least they showed his discrimination. His judgment of female excellence appeared to be as sound as his scientific attainments were brilliant.

Leading through strength to weakness, she directed the conversation back to the news of Saxton doings, and of her own home, careless of the openings it gave for the pleas or allusions which she had prohibited. She appeared to be too interested in the resulting conversation to notice their approach to No. 13 till they were directly before it. "I mustn't be seen standing here," she said hurriedly. She was gone up the steps.

Lord Britleigh looked round for a taxi, feeling that he had done rather well. A good deal better than he had feared. Such delusions are common enough among those who have just engaged in single combat with a woman's tongue. After a few hours doubts may grow.

Miss Merivale went to her room. It is sometimes necessary to chronicle that of which we cannot approve. She lit a cigarette (Lady Barbara prohibited smoking, except by men, and in the basement only. A low place for a low thing); she lay back in a very comfortable chair; she put slim grey heels on the dressing-table. Her delusion was that she could think especially well in that attitude. It is less a question for us than for the medical profession. It may have sent blood to the brain.

She reflected that the Calthorpe Garage is open all night. She could get either of Lady Barbara's cars out when she would. The Morris-Oxford would do. The only problem would be to leave the house and get back unobserved. The front door would be useless. It had two locks, two bolts, and a chain. Heavyweights all. It would have been difficult to open it in the night-silence without being heard at the other side of the square. Nobody ever inquired why it was secured in this manner. No one having any secret or hostile purpose was likely to approach the house by its central publicity. But Lady Barbara might have had a stroke had she learnt that the butler had retired without securing it in this fivefold way. It was ceremonial. An atavistic instinct.

But it is not necessary to leave a house by the front door, even in Belleville Gardens. There was a door in the basement of a more reticent kind, and of a superior modesty. A door that was content with a single bolt of a lighter pattern, and a lock in which the key was always left, and in which it turned very easily. It was a fact though Miss Merivale was not aware of this circumstance—again I chronicle that of which it is impossible to approve—that on many nights it was not fastened at all.

She decided that she could leave the house and return without difficulty. It would be rather a game.

CHAPTER X.

IT was early on the Thursday morning following the events already recorded that Percy Timmins, a boy employed by the Neverfail Dairy Co., of St. John's Road, was pushing his delivery barrow along the edge of the Bell Street pavement when he noticed something which caused him to stop whistling, let down the handles of the barrow, and approach the door of No. 30 with a pleasant consciousness of excitement and mouth and eyes open to about an equal width.

The street was not then fully light, though the lamps had been extinguished. The morning was damp and misty, the pavement slippery, with a hint of freezing. What the boy saw was the dark line of a stream of blood which had flowed under the ill-fitting door, formed a little pool in a hollow of the step, and then poured over to spread widely upon the blue-brick pavement beneath it.

The boy said "Golly!" as to the exact meaning of which I am not as clear as I should like to be, and after a moment's pause mounted the step, and made a successful attempt to look through the letter-box without treading in the blood. He looked upon the drab walls of an empty interior, and upon a portion of thin banisters, once painted green, and some uncarpeted stairs. He could not look down low enough to observe the source of the stream which had excited his attention. He gave up the attempt quite as soon as could reasonably be expected. But he stood for some time after that in uncertainty as to what his next action ought to be. At that early hour the street was empty, and he could not regard his responsibility for his employer's milk as less than that for a stranger's blood, which was already spilt. He looked round for a policeman who was not there. He hesitated as to whether he ought to knock upon the house door to inform the occupants of the unusual nature of its output. The glance he had had at the interior did not encourage him to expect any reply. If (as he may have been disposed to hope) it was a case of murder, he might not be well received should he knock up the murderer to inform him of the untidiness of his operations. He considered knocking up the next door neighbour, and the thought reminded him that he had to make a delivery only four doors farther on, to one of those cautious customers who are not content for the bottle to be put outside the door to demonstrate the general honesty of the race. There he could both continue to perform his duty and find the relief of confiding his discovery to others. He picked up the handles of his barrow and pushed on.

But he paused before the door of No. 38; he was aware of the approach of the heavy and deliberate steps of Police Constable Robbins, for whom he waited, and for whose benefit he pointed an eager finger along the pavement, as he said in a voice that trembled with a natural excitement, "Please, sir, there's someone a-bleeding out of that door."

Police Constable Robbins, somewhat quickening his step, but without abandoning his dignity, approached the door which was indicated, and made an exclamation very similar to that which Percy had already contributed, but of a less certain articulation. After this preliminary he acted with a prompt decision, rapping sharply with imperious knuckles upon a door that shook beneath the impact, and producing a hollow echo from the empty interior. There was no other answer, and his next exercise of authority was a stern "Stand back there" to a crowd of seven persons who had already collected, and who would be ten times that number in the next three minutes.

The constable, a young officer of only six months' experience, and with a hitherto unblemished record, may be excused if he gave a moment's thought to his next proceeding. The London constabulary receive very detailed instructions concerning the bewildering number of restrictions which are placed upon its citizens, of innumerable national laws and local regulations, and the correspondingly numerous occasions on which there may be legitimate interference with the freedom of their activities. They are also instructed with an even greater emphasis upon the few remaining rights and liberties which these citizens retain, probably because an overworked Parliament has not yet found time to deprive them of them. Among the last (which are too few to be easily forgotten) Constable Robbins knew that he must be cautious in entering any residential tenement without the permission of its lawful owner. Of course, in a case of murder, or even of suicide either achieved or attempted, his duty was clear, but there was not evidence here that there had even been an effusion of human blood. The rights (if any) or a London citizen to distribute the blood of one of the larger quadrupeds, either by negligence or design, under an ill-fitting front door in the early hours of a winter morning was a subject on which he had received no specific guidance, and he may have acted wisely, in addition to demonstrating the probability that we are evolved from a common ancestor, when he repeated the action of Percy Timmins, and applied his eyes to the letter-box. Sixteen inches of superior height enabling him to observe the interior from a different angle, exposed a fact which had been hidden from Percy's investigation. The lower part of the banister had been broken apart, and now leaned crazily across the hall.

He saw nothing to indicate that this was the result of any recent violence, and in strict logic it revealed nothing concerning anyone but the landlord and tenant (even eliminating the possibility of the occupation by a man of his own freehold), and I chronicle rather than explain that the sight aroused him to instant and decisive action. His whistle sounded along the street. He knocked again with additional vigour. He put a shoulder to the door, which caused its top bolt to give way. He would have burst it very easily but that the step gave him no means of using his weight to advantage, and he imitated Percy again in avoiding the central puddle. He was considering the probable effect of a good kick when the six-foot-four of Sergeant Middleditch came rapidly down the street.

> As waves before the bark divide,
> The crowd gave way before his stride,

as the poet expressed it very appositely about a century earlier. He took in the position with one Napoleonic glance. The crowd drew back at his curt order at least six inches further than they had done for Constable Robbins.

"You don't know what is behind that door, Robbins, what it might drop back onto. The window's the way." The window looked flimsy enough, though there were wooden shutters within it which might offer a more formidable resistance. But they collapsed very quickly before the resolute and well-directed staves of two policemen.

"You'd better come with me, Robbins," said the sergeant. There were two other constables on the scene now, to provide the necessary official atmosphere to the street scene, though they were not sufficient to check the operations of Sneaky Sanders, who took his harvest unseen from the pockets of the outer fringe of the gathering crowd.

There were two long minutes of waiting silence, and then the door did not open, but the sergeant appeared at the broken window. "Atkins," he called out, "you'd better phone the station. Tell the Inspector there's murder here, and I'll wait till he arrives."

CHAPTER XI.

IT was during the afternoon of the same day that Chief Detective-Inspector Combridge entered a quiet restaurant in the neighbourhood of Moorgate Street Station and took a seat in its dustiest corner, where he remained for over an hour with no more excuse than the pot of tea and plate of half-eaten bread-and-butter before him.

Not to excite anticipations that will not be realized, it is necessary to say at once that he was not watching for anyone. He had no subtle purpose in mind beyond the desire to think quietly over the facts regarding the Bell Street murder which he had ascertained already, and experience had taught him that there was no place where this could be done with greater security against interruption than in any one of London's innumerable tea-shops.

He had no reason to complain of the conditions under which the problem had been presented to him. He had been summoned promptly from Scotland Yard by the inspector at the local station, who had acted in such a way that no clues had been lost, no traces blurred. He had the services of one of the most intelligent police forces in the world, a dozen of whom had already been detailed to obtain information he had required. His only handicap was the absence of the gifted amateur who usually appears on these occasions to assist the dullness of the official mind.

He already knew a good deal. The murdered man was almost certainly either Wilfrid or Dudley Ralston—

probably the latter. The house had been occupied, or used, by these brothers in a very singular way. There were evidences that the front door had not been open for a long period. They had preferred to approach it from a back entry in River Street, through a door which had quite recently been strengthened by a heavy lock. The house (or at least parts of it) had been equipped with heat and light from the public supplies, but no inspector had entered it to take the states of meters which were not there. Gas and electric currents had been illicitly tapped, probably to prevent such intrusions upon a degree of privacy which could hardly have been desired for any lawful purpose. There was a telephone instrument, but the number had been kept out of the directory, and the account had been covered by a needlessly large deposit, paid under the pretext that the tenant might be away for uncertain periods and did not wish to risk disconnection. Inquiry showed that it had been used quite recently, but very little, unless for incoming calls, of which there would be no record. The rent was paid by the year in advance. All these transactions were in the name of, and had presumably been carried out by, Mr. Dudley Ralston, who now (if it were he) lay in the public mortuary with his head nearly separated from his body, and other injuries.

He had already ascertained that Mr. Dudley Ralston had had a banking account at the East Grinstead branch of the London and Northern, at which there was a credit balance of £437 3s. 5d. Very large sums had been passed through this account, mostly by cash credits and cheques drawn to self, so that it might be difficult to follow these transactions. Still, there might be something to be learnt there. In a couple of hours a clerk would arrive from that bank who would be able to say definitely if the corpse had been rightly identified as Dudley Ralston.

There were some singular internal features about the way in which the house had been occupied. There was very meagre sleeping accommodation. There were absolutely no evidences of female occupation, nor of any suitable provision for such a contingency. The furnished rooms were so selected that their occupation was unlikely to be observed. There was one of the largest that had been fitted up as a workshop or laboratory, but for a purpose which the Inspector had been unable to determine, and which he felt might supply the key to many of these sinister circumstances, though he recognized that it might fall short of the evidence which would be necessary to identify and convict the murderer. There was a very curious fact which (he thought) could hardly fail to be helpful in the final elucidation of the crime. It was due to the keen eyes of Sergeant Middleditch that it had been observed that a dark thread had been stretched across this door, which had been locked, and which had been opened by a key from the dead man's pocket.

Upon the facts as he had them—and it must be evident that he had not been idle to have learnt so much in the few hours which had elapsed since he had been called to the scene—suspicion centred upon the brother who had been, as far as was known, the only other occupant of the house. To find and interview him was, in any case, the first and obvious necessity. If he were innocent and unaware of the crime, it was not probable that they would have long to wait before he should return to the house. For this contingency the back door had been left locked in the usual way, and (apparently) unwatched and unguarded. If Wilfrid Ralston should enter by that way, he would find that his exit might be a more difficult matter. If he did not return, he would go very near to pleading guilty by the mere fact of his continued absence. At least, so it would have been had it been possible to keep such a crime from the publicity of the daily Press. As it was—well, there were two sides even to that. An appeal to the brother could be made through those channels which could hardly fail to reach him, or an appeal to others to come forward with information concerning him.

For that was the Inspector's real difficulty. All that he knew of the second brother was from such documentary evidence as the house and the dead man's pockets had held. Of where he lived, of his appearance, of his occupation, he had no information whatever. His knowledge of the laws of evidence told him that the question of identification might be a very difficult one, unless the scales of chance should incline in the direction of justice, as they often will.

CHAPTER XII.

IT WAS after eight that evening, and Inspector Combridge was about to leave his office at Scotland Yard. He had just telephoned to Bell Street and ascertained that there had been no visitors to the scene of the murder; and given instructions that he should be rung up at his private number at any hour during the night should there be any development, when his desk instrument rang, and he turned back to receive the information that Mr. Wilfrid Ralston had called in reference to the "murder in River Street."

"River Street?" he said to himself. "Yes, of course. That's how he thinks of the place. He used to get in by the back entry. Yes, send him up, and let Fordyce know that I want him here to take down."

Two minutes later Mr. Ralston was shown into the room. He held an *Evening News* in his hand, and was plainly agitated. The keen and experienced eye of Inspector Combridge judged that the agitation was genuine. He inclined to the opinion that it was the result of a recent shock as he had come upon the newspaper report. If so, Mr. Wilfrid Ralston was innocent of the crime, or of any participation in it, and he must look farther afield. Perhaps the agitation were even a little excessive, unless for a brother who was very dearly loved. It may be difficult to judge fairly of the previous attractions of a man who is first observed when his head is hanging from his body at an acute angle, but, after allowing for this circumstance, Inspector Combridge still thought Mr. Dudley to have been unlikely to inspire any overwhelming affection.

The Inspector did not introduce himself or offer his hand, as he indicated a chair at the farther side of his rather wide table, and said courteously, "Mr. Wilfrid Ralston? I take it that you are the brother of the unfortunate man who was murdered in Bell Street this morning? It is good of you to come to see us so promptly." He spoke slowly and quietly, giving his visitor time to get his breath, and to re-gain the self-control which appeared to have faltered as he entered the room, but Mr. Ralston was quick in his reply. "I've only read it during the last ten minutes. I picked it up in a tea-shop in the Strand." He looked down the paper he held. "I suppose you're quite sure? It really *is* Dudley?"

"He was identified by a cashier from his bankers about an hour ago."

"Can you tell me anything more than there is here? I know that everything doesn't always get to the Press. Is it a case of burglary? Did the rooms seem upset?"

"There was some confusion in the upstairs room—the one that appeared to be in most general use."

"There was a locked room on the other side of the landing. I hope it has not been interfered with in any way?"

"We naturally searched the premises. We should not have stopped for a locked door under such circumstances. The room you mention had no indication of having been entered previously, if you mean that. In fact, the thread was still there."

Mr. Ralston looked relieved at this information. He also looked puzzled. "The thread?" he said vaguely.

The Inspector had a moment of silence. Up to this point he had answered his visitor's questions, knowing that he was learning at least as much by this means as he would have been likely to do by reversing the process, but he had no intention of letting the control of the interview pass out of his hands. Beside that, there was an etiquette to be observed in these matters, and as is often the case with those who are entirely merciless, he was scrupulous to observe the rules of the game.

"Mr. Ralston," he said, "I appreciate your action in calling upon us, and it is only fair that I should put the case from the official standpoint before we go further. A murder has been committed—there is no possible doubt of that—in a house to which you and the murdered man appear to have been the only ones who had legitimate access. It is, as I am sure you will appreciate, a somewhat singular establishment. It has some features which would excite the curiosity of those who might observe them under any circumstances—features which we are now bound to investigate. Primarily, we have to look for the murderer. Till we can place him with certainty, we are bound to exercise a general suspicion. I am not suggesting that you are in any way responsible for your brother's death when I warn you that anything you say is at your own risk, and might be used against you in evidence. You are under no obligation to incriminate yourself in any way. But, having said that, I assume that you have come to us as one who wishes to probe the cause of his brother's murder, and who recognizes the public duty of every citizen to assist such an inquiry. I am sure that you can give us very valuable assistance, and we shall be grateful for it. If there are any circumstances of an unfortunate or illegal character in connection with the uses to which the house has been put, for which you or your brother, or both of you, may have been responsible—circumstances which may or may not be directly connected with the crime—the same warning applies, but I would suggest to you that it may still be the wisest as well as the most proper course to take us into confidence fully, rather than that we should be left to make discoveries in other ways."

Mr. Ralston listened attentively to these observations, which did not appear to perturb him. Rather his original agitation appeared to have subsided, and it was with a return to his more natural manner that he answered, "As to what's happened to Dudley, I'll tell you at once that I know no more than you do. Probably less. I don't mind giving you all the information I can, and I haven't got anything to incriminate myself about. If I ask for any favours from you it will be in a different way. What I'm most concerned about is to know that my room has not been disturbed. I don't mean that I'm not concerned that my brother's dead, but when you understand more...well, you'll understand how I feel. What's this about a thread?"

Inspector Combridge noticed a change in his visitor's manner, and was aware that, with the assurance of innocence that he received, his own suspicions were inclined to rise. Mr. Ralston's mere self-possessed manner did not inspire confidence in a mind that was accustomed to opposing itself to others that were adroit and cunning in many dangerous and criminal ways. He still did not think that he had the murderer before him, but he was less than sure of his innocence, much less than sure of his freedom from other forms of illegality in connection with the Bell Street premises, and glad to think of the caution that had restrained his hand when Mr. Ralston had entered. Twenty years ago he would always have shaken hands under such circumstances, thinking that visitors to a police office should be put at their ease, and that everyone should be regarded as innocent till there was evidence against them. He could remember instances when he had found it quite awkward, even for him, to withdraw from an established friendliness of manner when it had become necessary. But in these days he had learnt a different habit. There were many with whom he shook hands at a final interview—few or none on a first introduction in connection with any criminal investigation who experienced that familiarity.

Now he observed that he was being interrogated again, and though he did not object to answer he framed his reply so that he should establish what he regarded as a more satisfactory procedure.

"There was a black thread stretched across the outside of the door in which you appear to be particularly interested, such as was not easy to see in the half-darkness of the landing, and was so fine that it would snap at a touch.

"It had obviously been placed in that position so that no one could enter or leave the room without breaking it. If you were unaware of it being there, and the house was used only by your brother and yourself, can you suggest why he should have put it there without your knowledge?"

Mr. Ralston thought for a moment before answering. "I was liable to use the room when he was absent. It was a method by which he would know whether I had been there. But I don't know why he should go to that trouble, nor of any other reason, legitimate or otherwise, that he could have had."

"Did he usually keep that door locked?"

"The room was let to me. I always kept it locked when I was away."

"The key was in your brother's pocket."

Mr. Ralston looked incredulous. He felt in his own, and drew it out. "You're wrong about that, anyway. I've got it here now."

"Then there are two."

Mr. Ralston was silent again. The key was not one which could be casually duplicated. Dudley had been explicit in his statement that he had only one. There were obvious inferences.

The Inspector was speaking again. He left the subject of the two keys. "Do you mind telling me for what purpose you and your brother used the house?"

"I didn't use it. I rented the one room upstairs from him for some scientific experiments which I wished to carry out privately."

"Were they of such a nature as to render it desirable that you should get the gas and electricity that you needed by illicit means? Your brother was not so short of money that he could not have paid the bills in the ordinary way."

Mr. Ralston showed a surprise which the Inspector was again inclined to consider genuine, though again he was not quite sure. "I didn't want any. At least, of course, there was a light in the room. I didn't use any power. I never gave it a thought."

"Can you tell me for what purpose your brother used the house in this singular way?"

"No. I can't. He didn't seem to use it much at all, as far as I observed. He gave me a key of the back door, and I went in and out as I liked. He wasn't often there."

"Did he have any caller that you could identify?"

"I never knew him to have any."

"There is a telephone. Was it for your use or his?"

"Not for mine. It was there when I first rented the room. I have never used it at all. I tried to ring him up once, and couldn't find the number in the directory."

"No, you wouldn't do that, because it's not there. Did you never hear him use the phone either?"

"I never heard him ring anyone up. He was rung up by someone once when I was there."

"Man or woman?"

"A woman, I think. I remember hearing a woman's name. A Jewish sort of name. Miriam. No—Myra."

"Can you recollect anything of the conversation? Did it sound like a personal or merely a business one?"

"I couldn't say definitely. My impression was of a business conversation with someone with whom a considerable intimacy existed. But it was of too general a character for me to say more than that. I remember an impression at the time that he did not wish me to hear...that he was trying to close the conversation all the time, and yet did not want to give the impression that anyone was with him."

The Inspector realized that his questions were being answered readily, and with some degree of freedom. His tone was nearer to geniality when he spoke again.

"Do you mind telling me the nature of the experiments on which you were occupied?"

"They were in connection with cinema apparatus."

The tone had become curter, and the Inspector put the thought that was in his mind in a more explicit and yet in a more general way.

"You see, Mr. Ralston, what we're up against in this. When a man is found murdered there's usually one or two things behind it—money or women. When a house is used in the rather queer way in which this one seems to have been, the explanation's usually to be found in one or other of the same directions. When you get the two things together—such a murder in such a house—it's most likely that if you get to the bottom of one, you're at the bottom of both. Now, we haven't been long on this case, but we've found out a good deal since this morning, and by this time tomorrow I expect we shall know some more. We know that your brother had very comfortable rooms in East Grinstead and a comfortable banking account in the same place. We've got to find out why he was in 30 Bell Street last night, and who murdered him there. If we find out why he paid the rent of that house, and what use it could be to anyone, shut up as it was, we mayn't be exactly home, but we're probably a long way on the right road.

"Now, you say that you used part of it for some private experiments of your own, but on your own account it wasn't taken for them. Very well. If we credit that, we've got to look elsewhere, and the sooner we start the better.

"But we have to check everything in these investigations—everything in its turn—and if you're sure that what you've been doing in that room had nothing to do with your brother's death, well, I want you to make me equally certain. You've told me as plainly as though you'd spoken aloud that he had a key of your room that you don't reckon he'd got any right to have, and there may have been other things going on that you didn't guess...but don't you think you might guess a bit now? I should like to know first whether he was in your confidence, and how far. Could he have given you away, or rather have sold you, if he had been willing to do so? Are these experiments of any commercial value? Or ever likely to be so? I'm sure you'll see how you can help me, if you like. I don't want to waste time on a false scent."

"There are some of those questions," Mr. Ralston replied, "that I can't answer, and some that I can; but I'll tell you one thing in a word that you couldn't have learnt elsewhere, and you'll understand more or less how I feel. I've developed a secret process in that room that I'm to sell at eleven o'clock tomorrow for a million pounds. That is, if the report of this murder doesn't queer the pitch."

The Inspector was not easily startled, nor of a very credulous disposition. His face gave no sign of how he regarded this information as he asked laconically, "Cash down?"

"No, not for a month. But I know just where I am, and if the agreement's signed the cash follows. I've only got to hand over the formula, and give a demonstration that's quite easy to do."

"Why should this murder queer your pitch?"

"I don't say that it will, but I'm dealing with a queer crowd, and suppose they thought that the formula might have gone into other hands. I haven't had time to think it out myself yet...it might mean delay at the best."

"Can it have been stolen?"

"No. I don't see how. I'm not really afraid of that. I only want the deal to go through."

"Did your brother know of the value which—which you put upon this invention?"

"Yes. But I don't see how he could have sold me all the same. He might have thought that he could, though I don't see how. I'll tell you what I'll do. I want this business of tomorrow morning off my mind, and I'll come back at midday, when I've thought things over more than I can all at once, and give you all the help that I can."

"Where is this appointment tomorrow?"

"At the offices of Vantons, Ltd."

"Very well. You had better leave me your address."

"I think I'll keep that to myself. I don't give it to anyone just at present."

"I'm afraid you must make an exception."

"And I'm afraid I must decline."

"We can find it easily enough. You simply prejudice yourself if you refuse."

"I don't think you could. Not tonight, anyway. I'll go to a hotel, if you like. Which do you recommend?"

"That's for you to choose."

"Very well. We'll say the Gardiner."

Mr. Ralston, an observant man, rose without offering his hand, said goodnight to the Inspector, nodded casually to the officer who had been quietly recording the conversation at an adjoining table, and went his way.

The Inspector showed the soundness of his judgment in not troubling to have him followed. He had no doubt that he would spend the night at the Gardiner, if a room were available there, and that he would be punctual at his appointment at Vantons. What he said was, "You'd better have your notes transcribed for nine in the morning, Fordyce. I shall want to go over them first thing when I come in. And I want the records of Vantons' directors looked up. They're a queer bunch, if I'm not mistaken. There's not much that one or two of them wouldn't do for a good deal less than a million pounds."

CHAPTER XIII.

MR WILFRID RALSTON attended punctually at eleven the next morning at the offices of Vantons, Ltd., accompanied by his solicitor, Mr. Jellipot, a very capable man who specialized in certain departments of commercial and patent law. There is no reason to doubt the soundness of his advice or the value of his assistance at both this and other stages of the negotiation, but a detailed consideration of these issues is outside the scope of the present narrative.

They were kept waiting, with a visit of apology from Mr. Sinfield, for nearly half an hour, during which time Mr. Ralston might have been excused had some symptoms of nervousness developed. But he took it coolly enough, only asking permission, toward the end of the time, to telephone to Inspector Combridge to inform him of the delay he was experiencing. Having made a definite appointment to be at Scotland Yard at 3:15 P.M., he showed no further sign of impatience till Mr. Sinfield came with renewed apologies to say that the Board was now ready to receive them.

Being seated at the foot of the table, round which were now gathered the whole of Vantons' directors, together with the two eminent lawyers who were retained to deal with such matters as were now before them, Mr. Ralston had a short moment in which to observe or imagine an atmosphere of restrained excitement or curiosity, before he must concentrate his attention upon the fact that the

Chairman, with not more than the customary circumlocution, was informing him of the decision of the Board, in view of the "tragic and most inopportune occurrence, of which it would be foolish of any of us to profess that we are not cognizant."

"A fortnight ago," he went on, in the voice of important wheeziness with which we are already familiar, "we met here to consider one of the most amazing claims which has been made in the course of the scientific developments of the last fifty years. It was a claim that might have been dismissed as an absurdity without any serious examination, but the course of the developments to which I have alluded has been such as to demonstrate that nothing should be dismissed on such grounds, or in such a way, and it has been the boast of this firm that it examines everything that is brought before it with patient and impartial care.

"The result of this attitude was that you, Mr. Ralston, were able to give us a demonstration of a most interesting character—a demonstration that went far to support the claim which you had made. We subsequently considered the matter, and we came to the conclusion that, if you can do what you say, it must prove to be an invention of enormous value. We say frankly that we are of that opinion; and thinking as we do, we did not haggle over the price. We accepted your own figure, and we appointed this morning to agree—and perhaps to sign—an agreement embodying the sale and purchase of the formula you have discovered.

"It is only this morning that we have officially learned—it was known to some of us yesterday—that an incident has taken place—if I may call it an incident—that a crime has been committed on the very premises where your experiments have been conducted—that your own brother has lost his life—and while we recognize every possibility—while we appreciate that there may be nothing here but a tragic coincidence—you will admit, as a business man, that there is a probability that this occurrence may have a connection with the guarding or betrayal of the very valuable secret which we must suppose that that room contained.

"Now, Mr. Ralston, it is not our habit—it is not consistent with our reputation—to draw back from a bargain which we have made even though the legal formalities may be incomplete—without strong and certain reason for the adoption of such a course, and after full consideration our decision is this."

Mr. Levinstein's speech, which had been of a somewhat jerky construction as he had prepared the ground with these preliminary observations, became firm and lucid as he entered upon the decision to which it led.

"We have decided to offer you the agreement in the form in which it had been already drafted, without modification. This agreement contains certain clauses which had been considered necessary by our legal advisers, dealing with the alternate possibilities of patent rights or secret process, on which we cannot arrive at a final decision until the full facts are in our possession, but they are such as, I feel sure, your own solicitor will accept as reasonable. They have no relation to the events of yesterday.

"In coming to this decision we have been influenced by the assurance you gave us that the secret formula had not been committed to writing, nor communicated to others. You will appreciate that this is, at present, no more than a verbal statement. We shall require an endorsement of the agreement, stating this fact explicitly, and in such a way that our obligations are conditional thereto.

"You also told us very frankly that the secret substance of which your invention consists could be analysed and reproduced, if it should pass out of your control, and we had a demonstration of the precaution which you have observed to avert such a possibility. We shall require a for-

mal declaration, on the same terms, that none of this substance can have passed, and as a substantive fact that it has
not passed, at any time into the possession or control of
others.

"We shall also require an undertaking that the payment
of the purchase money will not be required in less than
three weeks from the successful demonstration on which
the purchase depends, but whether this, which may be
considered a minor point, involves any modification of the
agreement you will know better than I. How soon could
such a demonstration be given?"

Mr. Ralston had listened to these conditions with an
impassive face, having good reason for reluctance to accept, and seeing how prejudicial it would be to show hesitation concerning them. But the final question was one he
could easily answer.

"I could manage a satisfactory demonstration within
two days in my own laboratory, or within a week in any
premises you may prefer."

"We propose to leave the conditions under which the
demonstration will be made entirely in the hands of Professor Blinkwell. If he is satisfied that there is no objection
to it taking place in your own laboratory—"

The Professor said he thought that there would be no
objection which could not be overcome. The saving of
time was an important consideration. "I am sure," he
added courteously, with a smile to Mr. Ralston, "that we
shall be able to fix these matters up without difficulty."

It was at this point that Mr. Jellipot interposed. He had
considered the new conditions put forward, and he could
not see any valid objection to them. That is, providing that
Mr. Ralston's previous statements had not overrun the
facts of the case, in which event the objection to signing
them might be very strong indeed. He saw also that it
might be very difficult for his client to state his objection
in that event without prejudicing his position very seri-

ously. He said quietly, "I think, Mr. Chairman, with your consent, it might be well if I have a few words with Mr. Ralston privately. I should like him to be quite clear as to the effect of the new proposals which you have made, and to take my instructions from him. I don't suppose we shall delay you more than two or three minutes."

"Certainly, Mr. Jellipot," the Chairman answered. "Sinfield, you had better show them into your room."

"Jellipot, I'm not going to sign that," Mr. Ralston said definitely, as soon as they were alone.

"Then I'm afraid you'll find the deal's off—for the moment, anyway. What is the real objection? Could anyone have the formula? Particularly anyone who might give you away?"

"Suppose someone has it written down wrong, but so that they'd know how to put it right in their own minds?"

Mr. Jellipot looked doubtful. He did not waste words in asking whether such were the case. He said, "It would be a question of construction—of the exact wording of the clause. It's the sort of point that goes to the House of Lords when such a sum is at issue. If there's a serious risk, I can't advise you to take it. But you know best about that. Of course, I'll bear it in mind when we're wording the clause. Is it a man or a woman? Anyone you can really trust?"

"It's a woman. I—hardly know that."

Mr. Ralston looked what he was—a very troubled man.

"You don't think they've got it now?" It occurred to Mr. Jellipot's active mind that the agreement might be no more than an elaborate trap. That Vantons, Ltd. might have already possessed itself of the formula by illicit means, and that this endorsement of the agreement was only intended to draw his client into a false declaration which would make it more difficult for him to proceed against them when he discovered the truth.

He put this possibility in discreet words.

Mr. Ralston shook his head. No, it wasn't that.

Mr. Jellipot was puzzled. If Mr. Ralston, he thought, had let the formula pass, in whatever form, into the hands of a woman of whom he was less than sure....

Mr. Ralston would have liked to say that it was one of whom he had been sure—absolutely—till yesterday, and that he was still sure of her up to that date. But it came so near to the explanation of other things which he must forget. His mind was fixed on one thing. He *had not been* to River Street on Wednesday night. Had not been there at all. He would remember nothing contrary to that.

Mr. Jellipot said at last, "Well, I can't advise in the dark. I don't ask you to say more. It's up to you to decide. There's one stipulation we might make. We might delay the actual handing over of the formula till they've satisfied themselves with the demonstration, or even till they're prepared to complete. It saves any possibility that they might put up some dummy to say he had the formula from you—and that's a real risk. It gives us something to show, too, for the time we've been talking here."

"Very well," Mr. Ralston answered, "we'll go ahead on those lines." Even if there were any risk—and he didn't think there was much—it wouldn't get less by delay. And there looked like being trouble enough, without this falling through now. They went back to the boardroom.

There were two or three voices talking together that fell to silence as Mr. Jellipot opened the door. Mr. Ramsbottom's, continuing a second longer that the others, could be heard distinctly, "...if they haven't run him in before then, and that's a...." Mr. Jellipot had no difficulty in understanding. He had the same thought at the back of his own mind, but he had to keep it in that retirement. He could not say to his client, "Of course, I'm calculating all the time, in your interests, how these matters will stand if you should be arrested tomorrow for murdering your brother."

What he did say was, "I have advised my client, Mr. Chairman, that there can be no reasonable objection to the conditions you have proposed, providing that you agree to a modification which almost logically follows, and to which I feel sure there can be no objection, and that is that the formula shall not be disclosed until you have expressed yourselves satisfied with the demonstration and are prepared to purchase. The purchase money will then be deposited in exchange for the formula, on such terms as will enable you to prove that it is that which it purports to be before it is actually paid over."

"I fail to see—" Mr. Levinstein began.

"Well, I will put it plainly, and I feel sure you will excuse my bluntness. I am bound to protect my client against every eventuality in a deal of this magnitude. If the formula were handed over to you, it is natural to suppose that you would take sufficient precaution against its going out of your possession before patent protection had been obtained, but the fact remains that it would be possible—theoretically possible—for it to be communicated to an outside party, and if such a one were to say that he had received it from my client, under whatever circumstances, and at whatever date, it might be difficult for him to disprove. I cannot advise a course by which he might be placed in the position of having to prove a negative before he could claim his rights."

The Chairman looked at his colleagues, but no one spoke. There had, in fact, been delicate suggestions of such a development among them during the last five minutes. Mr. Ramsbottom had gone beyond that. Now they sat in silence, leaving Mr. Levinstein to deal with the position in his own way.

He said, "Well, it shall be as you wish—if our legal advisers approve. You know our mind, Mr. Winterton. If you and Mr. Samuels will agree to the draft with Mr. Jelli-pot, it shall be initialled before we part, and the fair copies can be exchanged this afternoon. That is how we do our business, Mr. Jellipot. When a thing is once settled it goes through at once. Professor Blinkwell, you might like a word with Mr. Ralston as to how this demonstration can be arranged."

CHAPTER XIV.

MR. RALSTON was at Scotland Yard at the appointed hour. He had lunched with Mr. Jellipot, and had taken that gentleman into his confidence on almost everything except the one all-important matter which he would not mention even to him. He had received in return a piece of advice which he realized had been meant for him, though it had been spoken with a general application only.

"The mistake most people make," Mr. Jellipot had remarked, "when they're being questioned by the police is that they pull themselves up too late. Nine times out of ten it pays to be frank, and in the tenth it pays best to say nothing at all; but hardly anyone does that. They go on talking about one thing after another, and think they're doing very well till they find they're on the edge of the pit, and when they try to turn they slip down—and there they are."

Mr. Ralston did not doubt the wisdom of this reflection. His difficulty was to apply it to his own case. He had a good nerve and a very acute brain, but he was suffering from the effects of a sleepless night and the strain of the morning's interview as he sat opposite to Inspector Combridge, whose manner was even more coldly official than it had been on the previous evening.

"Mr. Ralston," he began abruptly, "when did you last see your brother alive?"

Mr. Ralston had prepared himself for that question. He answered readily, "Last Saturday afternoon."

"When did you first hear of his death?"

The Inspector, watching with particular alertness for the way in which these interrogations were received, thought that there was a second of surprise, if not of hesitation. Perhaps it was natural enough. "I told you that yesterday. I picked up an *Evening News* while I was having tea, and when I read it I came straight here."

"Yes," said the Inspector thoughtfully, "so you did. I expect you'll be wanting to get back to your room to see that it's not been disturbed."

"I have made an appointment to meet Professor Blinkwell there this evening. I don't know what is the customary procedure in such cases, but I suppose I shall have no difficulty in obtaining possession of my room."

"None at all, so far as we are concerned. We have finished our examination, and removed one or two articles, in particular a section of banister which had been broken off at the foot of the front stairs. There is to be an inquest at 3:00 P.M. tomorrow. I've got a subpoena from the coroner to serve on you before you leave. On our present information your brother was unmarried and you are his next of kin. We have not learnt of a will. I suppose you know that he was a fairly rich man?"

"No. I knew practically nothing about his private affairs. I knew that he had an annuity of £250, but I thought that ceased at his death. I should be surprised if he had left anything apart from that."

"There are securities—mostly bearer bonds—for about £26,000 at his East Grinstead apartment." Mr. Ralston looked his astonishment. He had believed that his brother augmented his income considerably by the precarious methods of the racecourse and the card table, and possibly in less reputable ways. He had not been without a natural curiosity as to the use of the River Street house. He had had no idea of any such accumulation of solid investment.

"I may want to take a statement from you, but it can wait till after you've given evidence at the inquest tomorrow. It may not be necessary. Anyway, I needn't keep you now. Fordyce, you might see that Mr. Ralston has the keys of the Bell Street house before he leaves. He appears to be the legal representative of the dead man. Of course, you'll take a receipt."

Mr. Ralston left with a feeling of relief. The interview had been much shorter and easier than he had anticipated. Yet he was not entirely at ease. It was not only the shadow of that which he carried in his own mind. It was the impression of cold and ruthless efficiency which that office—which Inspector Combridge—gave. And how on earth had Dudley possessed himself of £26,000? He saw that there were solid business reasons why he should visit East Grinstead and take possession of that of which he appeared to be the legal heir. This was not a million pounds, but it was something tangible. Two days ago it would have been occasion for a fresh endeavour to persuade Miss Merivale to his purpose. But now...?

CHAPTER XV.

The office of coroner is a very ancient one. For many centuries it fulfilled an important duty in inquiring into all cases of violent or suspicious deaths, with some subordinate functions which do not concern us. The inauguration of the police force in the early part of last century introduced another authority, and tended to duplicate these proceedings, with waste of public money and time, and occasional hardship to accused or suspected persons.

The inauguration of the police force was an essential factor in the suppression of personal liberty which is embodied in the enormous mass of Parliamentary legislation of the last hundred years, and it is difficult to the modern mind to understand that English civilization could have existed for a millennium without feeling the need of a semi-military force which now numbers more than one out of every hundred of able-bodied males in the country, and is still said to be inadequate for the accumulation of repressive duties which have been laid upon it, and for the regulation of the slaughter which is permitted in the public roads.

This force could not now be disbanded without a radical change in national habits and character which would amount to a revolution, and, in the end, it is the office of coroner which is more likely to be abolished. In the meantime some minor changes in procedure and a system of compromise have established a working arrangement of a tolerable smoothness, and though Inspector Combridge was in no doubt that he could have managed better without the coroner's assistance, he was content that he could rely upon the co-operation of that official, and it was no surprise when he was told as he sat at his desk at about noon on Saturday morning, "There's the coroner's office on the phone, sir. I think Mr. Hastilow wants to speak to you himself."

He picked up the receiver. "Yes. Speaking. Good morning. Yes, so I thought. Oh, well, about the usual. Six anonymous letters this morning, and one signed that we are following up. We've two lines of inquiry that seem hopeful. Yes, that's what I told Sir Henry. It isn't these out-of-the-way cases that cause the most trouble. It's those that look simple that give the headaches. I've promised him an arrest within a week. Yes, I served it for you yesterday when he called. But I don't think you'd have had any trouble. Yes, but there's another reason. No, I don't think it is. Though I don't say he isn't capable. He's the sort that would plan well. If it is, it'll mean a fight. No, not from our point of view. Thanks, I thought you'd look at it in that way. Yes, they'll be there. I should be much obliged if you would."

"Fordyce," he said, as the conversation ended, "the inquest's at two-thirty. I don't suppose it'll take more than two hours. There's a man named Mills being brought here at five o'clock. I expect I shall be back before then, but if I'm not he must be kept. I don't want him questioned till I get back. Treat him well, but don't let him go...oh, no, he's a boot-repairer."

He went out to get a quiet lunch, during which his mind continued its efforts to reconstruct the crime. If only they could find Ringbolt! He had the advantage of several items of knowledge which have not yet come before us, but as they were not sufficient to enable his experienced mind to detect the criminal, or even to decide upon the motive which had caused the crime, it is unlikely that they would be more useful to us—even with the assistance of some facts of doubtful relevancy which are known to us, and of which he was not equally well informed.

After lunch he went on to the inquest. He did not expect to learn anything that he did not know, but you always have to be prepared for the unexpected, and he wished to observe the demeanour of Mr. Wilfrid Ralston in the witness-box. Before the day ended he expected to know a good deal more than would be disclosed in the coroner's court.

When he arrived the coroner was engaged in making some preliminary remarks to a jury who had just "viewed the body," and some of whom were feeling rather sick in consequence of that rather pointless ceremony. (But, of course, it prevents the possibility of a coroner with a sense of humour inventing a tragedy, and holding an inquest on a body that isn't there.) After that there was the evidence of Percy Timmins, and of the policemen in the order in which they had appeared upon the Bell Street premises, and then Sir Lionel Tipshift gave his account of the post-mortem which he had conducted upon the body of the murdered man.

The points of interest which emerged from this evidence may be briefly summarized. The body of Dudley Ralston had been found lying between the foot of the front stairs and the front door. It lay somewhat to the side of the stair-foot, in a pool of its own blood, the head having been almost completely severed. Part of the broken banister was beside and beneath it, and a large splinter of wood had penetrated between the second and third ribs on the right-hand side. A blow on the back of the head had fractured the base of the skull, and would of itself have been sufficient to cause death within a few hours. While it was possible that this might have been caused by a fall from the head of the stairs, Sir Lionel was of the opinion that it was at least highly improbable that it had been caused in that way. The wound was such as might be inflicted by a heavy, blunt instrument in the hand of a powerful man. It certainly occurred before death. Sir Lionel's opinion was that the blow had been the cause of the fall, or that after it had been inflicted Dudley Ralston's unconscious body had been thrown down the stairs. The body must have struck the banisters with great force where they turned at the foot of the stairs. It had not moved, or very little, after the splinter had entered the side. The head had been severed by a sharp curved blade, sickle-shaped, so that it had cut farther at either side than in the centre. Had it been a straight blade the head would have been completely cut off. There was no blood, nor any sign of a struggle, on the landing. It seemed certain that the fracture of the skull had been the earlier injury, and that the neck had been cut as Dudley Ralston had lain unconscious at the stair-foot, with the splinter penetrating his side.

It was during Sir Lionel's evidence that there occurred one of those outbursts of sudden contagious laughter which are always liable to break through the atmosphere of horror on such an occasion. There was a barman among the jury who may have taken more than a discreet minimum of the beverage which he dispensed, and who showed signs of an untimely somnolence as the case proceeded. At last an audible snore sounded through the court, and the man, being shaken by his colleagues to wakefulness, and rebuked by the coroner to a sufficient confusion, could be observed to be struggling manfully against a disposition to relapse into slumber. It was as Sir Lionel Tipshift explained the condition of the severed head that he slipped slightly in his seat, and recovered himself to be aware that all eyes were again upon him. It was doubtless from a natural desire to show that he was listening intelligently to the evidence that he convulsed the court by inquiring of the witness, with an aspect of owlish solemnity, *"Was he quite dead?"*

The remaining evidence was largely of a negative character. The murderer had left no trace. No weapon had been discovered. There was no sign of how he had entered or left the house. The front door had been secured on the inside. The lower windows were fastened in the same way. The only possible means of egress appeared to have been the back door, which was provided with a lock, a drop-latch, and a heavy bar which could only be put into position from the inside. This bar had not been put down, which was consistent with the murderer having left through that exit, and the drop-latch would act if the door were pulled from the outside. It had also been locked, and as no key had been found on the premises the presumption was that the murderer had taken the key and locked it from the outside.

There was nothing to indicate the motive for the murder, which did not appear to be robbery of an ordinary kind, as a sum of about £15 had been left in the pockets of the dead man, as had a watch of some value. The lower rooms of the house were empty and unfurnished. One of the rooms on the first floor, which appeared to have been in more or less regular use, was in some confusion, though not so as to give indication of any serious struggle. Another one, a laboratory used by the dead man's brother, had been left locked and undisturbed.

So much for the police evidence. Mr. Wilfrid Ralston was called, but he could throw no light on the tragedy. He rented a room in the house for some experiments of his own. Beyond that he did not know for what purpose his brother used it. Actually, he did not think he used it much for any purpose whatever. He had been there on the previous Saturday afternoon. That was the last time he had seen his brother alive. He did not know that he had any enemies, and could make no suggestion as to the cause of the tragedy. He had keys of the back door, which were still in his own possession. His brother had a duplicate set. Probably they were the only ones in existence. He could not say. So far as he knew, his brother and himself were the only ones who had legitimate access to the house. But his brother might have given permission to others without his knowledge. He could not say. The large lock had been put on the back door at his own request when he had taken the up-stair room. The drop-latch could easily have been forced. The bar was also fitted at his suggestion. He was conducting experiments of importance. He might wish to be undisturbed. Questioned as to what would have happened if he or his brother had required access while the other had barred the door, he replied that they rang in a way that was mutually understood. Questioned as to why the front door had not been strengthened in a similar manner, he replied that it was never used, and he had not considered it. He supposed that as there was no sign of occupation from the Bell Street side, and no one went in or out, that it would be very unlikely that anyone would be tempted to force an entrance there. Also, anything done there must be observed, as that door faced the street, whereas the other was in the retirement of the bending passage.

The coroner summed up briefly. That it was a case of murder could not be doubted. Suicide was impossible for obvious reasons. So was accident. So was manslaughter, in view of the terrible nature of the injuries inflicted. There was at present no due to the murderer, but the jury could be sure that the police were active, and it was improbable that the perpetrator of so brutal a crime would escape its penalty. Their own duty was clear. The verdict must be murder against some person or persons unknown.

The jury assented without retiring, and the inquest terminated without sensational revelation, such as it might have been hoped that it would provide.

CHAPTER XVI.

TITUS MILLS sat facing Inspector Combridge. He had his hat in his hands, and was turning it round incessantly. Presumably he derived some mental or physical comfort from this action, which, however, appeared to be of little assistance to a reluctant memory.

The Inspector waited in a patient silence. He had already been told, what he had already known, that Titus Mills occupied a house on the other side of River Street, almost opposite to the entrance of the one which had been the scene of the crime. It followed that Titus had been well placed for observation. It did not follow that he had observed.

He had come forward voluntarily to say that he could give information, and now that he was here to do so it amounted to no more than that he had seen a suspicious character hanging round the passage entrance on more than one occasion during the last month. He had seen him go up the entry a week or two ago, and seen Dudley Ralston go in later. Shortly after that the man had come out alone.

That was all. He could not remember the date. He would not be able to identify the man.

"Know a man named Ringbolt?" said the Inspector suddenly.

Mills looked blank. He shook his head.

"Well, you don't seem to know much. But you've done quite right to come. If you see the man again, don't let him out of your sight till you find out who he is, and where he lives. What else is there?"

He asked this because the man seemed as reluctant to go as to speak.

"Is it like as there'll be any reward offered?" he asked at last.

"Not for people whose memories can't come to life without it," the Inspector answered curtly. "Now sit down, Mills, and listen to me"—for the man at last showed signs of moving. "You can't remember which night that man went up to the entry, because you didn't see him at all. You daren't mention the day, because I might have found out that it was one of your late nights at Smith and Babcock's, as I daresay it was. By the way, I've had a note from Belinda Miggs. Who's she?"

The man sat silent, looking sullen and disappointed, and the Inspector went on. "Isn't she a bedridden aunt of yours who lies looking out of the upstairs window? Well, she seems to think she'd rather tell us herself than leave it to you. Don't I make a good guess when I say that it was she who saw Ring—this man hanging round? And perhaps a good deal more that she hasn't told even to you, when she found how you meant to use what she *did* tell? Now you can get home just as quick as you like, but unless you hurry you'll find that I'm there first. I've got a rather fast car."

Titus Mills went.

CHAPTER XVII.

IT was two days later—on Monday afternoon—that Mr. Ralston sat once more in the Inspector's room, facing him across the wide and neatly ordered desk, which was nearly bare except for a little heap of paid cheque-forms which he had been examining when his visitor was announced.

"Mr. Ralston," he said, "I've had a very busy week-end."

The tone was less conventional than the words, and Mr. Ralston responded curtly, "So have I." He was angry that he had been called away from the new demonstration that he was preparing, and in some anxiety as to the meaning of the urgent summons that he had received.

The Inspector selected one from the pile of cheques, and passed it over the table. "Seen that before?"

The cheque was dated October 19, 1929. It was drawn by Dudley Ralston to self or bearer, upon his own bank at East Grinstead. The signature had been cancelled in an ink of bluish tinge, and again in black. On the top left-hand corner, in the same bluish ink, it bore the words "Cancelled in error. J. J."

Mr. Ralston knew nothing of the cheque. He had never seen it before. In fact, he knew nothing whatever about his brother's banking arrangements. He had never had a cheque from him in his life, or even seen him draw one.

He said so, with relief in his voice. If he had been fetched here only for this.

The Inspector looked up, and the eyes of the two men met. He did not doubt that he was telling the truth. It was the reply which he had expected to get. "You think you are not interested in that cheque. Mr. Ralston, I hope it may save your life."

Mr. Ralston was startled. His eyes flickered, and became firm. "I did not know that it was in any danger."

"No? Well, I do."

The Inspector paused, but Mr. Ralston was on his guard now. He made no reply.

"Mr. Ralston, I'll be quite frank with you, and I'll come to the point at once. I haven't got a warrant, and I'm not sure that I've got enough evidence to justify me in applying for one. But I propose to detain you on suspicion of causing or being concerned in your brother's death."

Mr. Ralston came near to losing his self-control. He flushed angrily. "You can't do that. You've no legal right...."

"No? We won't discuss that. When we've talked it over a little further I think you'll agree. Mr. Jellipot? Yes, you can ring him up, if you like; but you'd better listen first. You'll have more to tell him when you do."

Mr. Ralston saw the advantage of listening. He sat down again in the chair from which he had risen in his excitement.

"I've told you," the Inspector went on, "that I'm going to treat you frankly, and, before we finish, you'll see why.

"First, as to the cheque. As you probably know, most of our London banks return the paid cheques with their customers' pass-books, and that's the end of them, as far as the banks are concerned. But the custom is not universal. Long after it became general in London, it was still the practice of Northern and Midland banks to claim that these cheques are their property, on which the customer has paid only the value of the stamp duty that is levied upon them. Among the London banks the London and Northern—which was originally a Lancashire bank—alone continues this practice, never returning a cheque to a customer unless a specific application be made. The cheques I have here are those which were drawn by your brother since he opened the account at East Grinstead two years ago. With the exception of the one I have shown you, they have proved useless. They are drawn to tradespeople, to brokers for the securities which your brother purchased, to self for cash which was taken in Treasury notes. The one you have seen was presented by a lady three months ago. She took Treasury notes in spite of the largeness of the amount. That, in itself, is significant, but not helpful. But the cancellation shows that it had been previously tendered at another bank. The cashier at East Grinstead remembers her explanation, and the hesitation with which he paid it. In fact, he declined to do so till he had telephoned your brother for his authority. She said that she had offered it in error over the counter of her own bank, and the cashier had cancelled the signature before he had observed the mistake.

"Now this shows several things. The cashier who made such a mistake must have known the lady, and been in the habit of cashing cheques she presented, so that he had automatically cancelled the signature even as his eyes fell upon it for what would have been the mere formality of observing its regularity. It is also evident that it must have been a cheque-form of the familiar colour and design, or he would have noticed the difference before he could have reached the point at which such an error could occur.

"We may, therefore, deduce that the cheque was cancelled in error by a cashier whose initials are J. J., and who is employed at one of the branches of the London and Northern Bank, and most probably within a very limited area. Such a cashier should be very easy to find. He will certainly know the lady, who can also be identified by the cashier at East Grinstead. It is at least a possibility that her name will prove to be Miriam or Myra, being the one who telephoned to your brother on the occasion when you were present."

"Myra," Mr. Ralston interjected.

"Very well, Myra. When we get in touch with this lady it is probable that we may learn more of your brother's occupations. Perhaps of the source of the considerable sum which he had accumulated, and of the use to which the house was put—matters on which we may have surmises, but on which, I will tell you frankly, we have at present no proofs.

"When we learn this I hope that it may give us some important light on the crime which we are investigating, and that it may be such as will clear you from the suspicion under which you now lie."

Mr. Ralston appeared to have gathered confidence as this explanation proceeded. He now said boldly, "I am absolutely without knowledge of, or concern in, the circumstances of my brother's death, and no one can be more anxious that the mystery should be cleared up. You have no cause to suspect me whatever, and I don't believe that you really do. I shall certainly resist any attempt to detain me here without a proper warrant with every possible legal resource."

He half rose again, but the Inspector continued, as though he had not observed the action.

"If you should be guilty of this murder, or of any complicity in it, the advice I am about to give you may be bad, and you will take it at your own peril. If you are innocent, I would urge you to be frank with me, in your own interest. It may avert the possibility—the very real possibility—that you may have to stand your trial as your brother's murderer.... Mr. Ralston, I will tell you some of the things which I already know.

"At about half-past eleven on Wednesday night—the night of the crime—your brother was seen to go up the passage to the River Street entrance of the house in which he must have been murdered during the next few hours. About an hour afterwards—or it may have been less—a small elderly man drove up in a taxi, paid it off, and also went up the passage. He came out again about twenty minutes later, and walked away. At about one you arrived on foot, and also went up the passage. Almost immediately afterwards a lady arrived alone in a private car, which she drove, and followed you in. She came out twenty minutes, or it may have been half an hour, later, in a state of obvious agitation and haste, and drove away. You left shortly afterwards, having presumably locked the door with your own key. As far as we know—as we have every reason to believe—you were the last man who was in the house in which your brother was murdered.... And when you were asked on this point you replied that you had not seen him since the previous Saturday."

"That," Mr. Ralston interpolated, "is the truth."

"The identification," the Inspector answered, unmoved, "leaves no doubt in my mind. If you are an innocent man, I ask you to tell me what happened in that house while you were in it, and who was the lady who called either upon yourself or your brother during that time."

"You forget, among other things, that I rented a single room in my brother's house, in which I had an occupation of absorbing interest. Even if I had been there that night—which I do not admit—it would be no reason for supposing that I was aware of everyone who came and went, or in any way concerned in a murder which might have taken place hours after I had left the house."

"I have not forgotten any of those things," the Inspector answered; "nor have I forgotten that the thread being unbroken across your door suggests that you may not have used your own room at all on that occasion."

97

"I have told you that I was not there."

"And I have told you that I am satisfied that you were. If you would tell me the name of the lady who left the house only a few minutes before you, you might do well for yourself, if you are an innocent man, and no harm to her, as in any case we shall have it within a few hours.... You may be interested to know that we have the number of the car she drove."

In saying this the Inspector deviated somewhat from the straight path of verbal accuracy. Mrs. Belinda Miggs had been able to do no more than to describe the car (somewhat vaguely), and to state that the last three numerals were 277. Still, the Inspector thought that should be sufficient.

Mr. Ralston was obviously perturbed. "You will gain nothing," he began, "from that...," and stopped in sudden realization of all that his remark implied.

"Well," the Inspector answered cheerfully, without appearing to notice anything, "We shall try. Had you any reason," he went on, "to think that your brother was selling you over?"

"He wasn't over-scrupulous," was the cautious answer, "but I don't think he was ever in a position to do so."

"Still, he might have tried? Did any of the directors of Vantons, Ltd., find their way to River Street?"

"Professor Blinkwell came on my invitation."

"Anyone else?"

"No."

"Not Nichols?"

"No. Certainly not."

"Well, he did. I quite expect it was he who saw your brother that night. That surprises you? Well, perhaps it's as well for you that it does. There might easily have been a quarrel over that, and a quarrel's easily begun, but it's not so easy to tell where it's going to end. Perhaps you'd be surprised to learn that there was an attempt to break into the house last night?"

Mr. Ralston had a right to look worried. He was engaged in preparing a demonstration which was (he hoped) to bring him a fortune, and he was doing this under circumstances which rendered it very difficult for him to protect his secret, which it was vital that he should do; he was under suspicion of a murder which he had not committed; he had just learnt that the Inspector was aware, with a disconcerting accuracy, of facts which he had hoped would remain undiscovered; he had been threatened with detention, if not arrest, at a moment when everything depended upon his freedom to complete the preparations in which he was engaged; and he was now informed that there had already been a night attempt (as he supposed) to discover the secret which he was protecting under such difficulties.

"I'm not much surprised at anything now," he said, truly enough. "I shouldn't even be surprised if I learnt that you'd failed to catch whoever they were, just as you're failing to find who murdered Dudley while you're keeping me here."

"Well," the Inspector answered, without loss of temper, "you're not so far wrong in that. My men failed me rather badly last night. But we may come out all right in the end.

"I understand how you feel, but you'd better just listen to me. You think if someone was trying to break into that house last night they were after this thing of yours, and it's likely enough, but it's not sure. There's something else about that house that you don't know, and I'm not sure that I do either, though I've got an idea. Now, if your brother's murder was something to do with this invention of yours, you may be in it or you may not, but if it was about something quite different, there's no one who's got more to gain than yourself if the truth is known; and if it's made public that we've made up our minds that it was your work, and they think we're settled down on the wrong scent—if it is wrong, which I don't say yet—we're likely to have a good deal less trouble than we otherwise should."

"You mean you want it to be said all over the place that you're detaining me on suspicion of murdering Dudley? Well, you're going too far. I might give you some help on my own terms, but they'd be rather different from that."

The Inspector pulled the drawer half open which was in the desk at his right side. It contained several documents which would have both surprised and interested Mr. Ralston. The top one was a warrant for his arrest dated May 3, 1928. It was in connection with a rather curious financial operation for which two other men had been tried and convicted. At that time Mr. Ralston could not be found. The case against him had been weaker than against the two who had been arrested, and after their convictions the third warrant had been allowed to lie in the office. Whether the recent mystery of his address had had any connection with this incident was best known to himself, but it was one which he doubtless regarded as a receding danger. The Inspector looked at the warrant, but he did not take it from the drawer. His mind turned to a document which was immediately beneath it. Observing it for ourselves, we must observe also that there had been some important reservations in the Inspector's frankness. It was a statement signed that morning by Mr. Nichols, giving his own account of his relations with Dudley Ralston and of his visit to River Street on that fatal night. If it were true, it was certain that Wilfrid Ralston had not murdered his brother during the interval between the times at which he had been seen by Mrs. Miggs to enter and leave the premises. *If....* And the details of that statement, unless upon the assumption that Mr. Nichols was himself the murderer—in which case it would be equally true that Mr. Ralston was innocent—would constitute an unlikely lie. But the Inspector's mind was not on that part of the statement, which he had already considered, and concerning the truth of which he had formed a definite opinion. It was upon its earlier portion, which dealt with Mr. Nichols' experience at 37 Willow Road, and other matters into which the Inspector would not have inquired, knowing nothing concerning them, but he had taken all that the gods had given him from the outpouring of a very frightened man. Perhaps also there may have been an impulse of malice in the mind of Mr. Joseph Nichols—a willingness to cause Mr. Ralston any possible trouble concerning an episode which had proved unprofitable to himself.

The Inspector did not regard it as relevant to the inquiry on which he was occupied, but experience had told him that you can never be sure. Anyway, it was a question easily asked, and would be an additional evidence to Mr. Ralston of the extent to which he was familiar with his private affairs.

"Who lives," he asked abruptly, "at 37 Willow Road?"

Mr. Ralston looked as surprised as the Inspector could desire, and then surprised him in turn by bursting into hearty laughter—perhaps the louder for the atmosphere of tension in which it came.

The sound of laughter ceased, but the amusement was still in Mr. Ralston's eyes as he answered, "Who lives at 37 Willow Road? I haven't the least idea."

"Then why," began Inspector Combridge, "should you give an address?"

"I used to pass Willow Road on the trams every morning, except Sundays, for about six years, and they used to stop just opposite where the name is put up."

"Then why…?"

"Oh, it just came to my mind. I thought he was watching me like a sneak-thief, and I gave him something to do."

"You mean it was just an address of which you knew nothing, written at random, to make a fool of the man who you expected to pick it up?"

"Yes. You're on the spot there. Did he try?"

The Inspector did not answer this question. He did not wish to be drawn into further explanation of the extent of his knowledge of Mr. Nichols' movements. But he felt that he had had the truth from both sides concerning this episode. They confirmed each other. It also confirmed his opinion of Mr. Ralston as a man of prompt and original ingenuities. He said, "There was a lady who helped you in this jest. Can you give me her name?"

"It would be of no assistance to you in this inquiry."

"Not Myra?"

"No."

"Not the lady who came to River Street in the night?"

Mr. Ralston was silent for one significant second. Then he said, "I have told you that the lady's name would be of no assistance to you in this inquiry."

"No?" said the Inspector. "But in view of the time you were in the house together it might be helpful to you."

Mr. Ralston did not rise to this bait. He had been thinking rapidly. He thought he saw a basis of cooperation which might be more satisfactory to himself, and even more helpful to the police, than that which the Inspector proposed. He said, "I've listened to you for a good while, now perhaps you'll listen to me."

That was a thing which the Inspector was very willing to do, but his telephone rang at the moment. He listened for some moments to a voice which was audible to Mr. Ralston, though that gentleman was annoyingly unable to hear the words. When the sound ceased Inspector Combridge said, "Tell Rollins that's good work." His face expressed his satisfaction. He looked at Mr. Ralston in calculating doubt, and then said deliberately, "Get me through to Lady Barbara Dillington."

CHAPTER XVIII.

LADY BARBARA DILLINGTON had a good library and a sound and somewhat eclectic taste in English literature. It was one of the regular duties of her secretary to read to her for half an hour every afternoon, during which period she would recline upon a couch in the drawing-room in an apparent slumber, which was sufficiently near to wakefulness to be aroused by any interruption of its routine.

During the five months that Miss Merivale had held her position this practice had introduced her to several books which are not in general demand at the lending libraries, but which are much less dull on a close acquaintance than she would have supposed them to be. On the afternoon of Monday, the 27th of January, 1930, she was occupied with a rather heavy volume of Robinson's *Ecclesiastical Researches*, and deriving, we may reasonably suppose, some satisfaction to herself from the curious scholarship, lucid thought, and admirable style of that too commonly disregarded author. She was reading:

> "Having taken this cursory view of the general state of adjacencies, and particular parts of Piedmont (for a part of it was in the diocese of Este, and all the Catholics in it were subject to the Bishop of Milan), and having observed that the country all round

was inhabited by dissidents, it may be proper
to descend into the valleys, and to search for
the apostolic Church of the French Protes-
tants...."

when there was the sound of the telephone bell in the adjoining room, which was separated only by a curtained
archway from the one in which she sat beside her employer's reclining form.

It was an unusual sound at this hour, during which it
was well understood that Lady Barbara was not to be disturbed for any casual reason.

"Miss Merivale," said that lady without opening her
eyes or altering her position, "you'd better see what it is."

Evelyn was conscious of a suddenly beating heart,
which had been aroused from its normal regularity during
the last few days by any unexpected incident, but she laid
down the book, even as she turned the page to encounter
the Four Considerations which naturally lead us to look for
religious dissidents in Piedmont.

She controlled her voice to its natural quietness as
Lady Barbara heard her say, "Yes, James. You should
have told them to wait. It's only about a dog. Very well,
put him through now. And James! We're running short of
coal here. You'd better see about it at once. You needn't
stay to listen in. Yes. No. I'm afraid you can't. Lady Barbara's lying down. It's her secretary speaking. Yes. Miss
Evelyn Merivale. No, we haven't lost a dog here. We don't
keep one. Very well, I'll write tonight. Yes. You can depend on that." She rang off.

"It's Scotland Yard," she volunteered, as she returned
to her employer's side, without writing for an inquiry
which she knew would have been otherwise inevitable.
"It's about a dog that's been stolen from about here.
They've been on the phone once before. Yes, I told them

I'd send them a line tonight to say that it's nothing to do with you."

"It hardly seems necessary," Lady Barbara remarked with reason. "But you'd better get it done before dinner, my dear, as you've said you will. Don't forget."

Evelyn said, "Oh, well, I suppose the police always are a bit fussy." She was quite sure that she wouldn't forget. She resumed her reading of the Four Considerations, but would have been very ill-equipped at the conclusion to pass an examination upon them. She was a young lady who had always despised mendacity as a resort of cowardice, and, behold! at this extremity the most practised liar might have been outpaced by the swift audacity of her invention. And then the necessary further lie that they had rung up before! or how could she have told James that she knew what it was about? And how quickly the policeman at the other end had understood the position! He must be quite used to such subterfuges. But she had got to be there tomorrow, or there was no telling what would happen. That had been quite clear from his voice. ("Yes, James, so there is," she heard herself saying, "but we can't risk running short on a day like this.") And suppose he wouldn't accept her explanation! Suppose it all came out in tomorrow's papers! Lady Barbara would have a—no, something worse than a fit. "...and the descendants of Berold," she was reading, "were called dogs for four hundred years."

"Dogs, my dear?" said the surprised voice of Lady Barbara, "Oh, *counts*! I thought it might have been *doges*. You seem to have that dog on the brain. Perhaps you'd better stop now, and get the letter off your mind."

CHAPTER XIX.

EVELYN sat opposite to Inspector Combridge at the desk with which we are becoming almost as familiar as himself, and Sergeant Fordyce was exercising his pencil in the strategically unobtrusive position which he occupied at a smaller desk somewhat to her right rear.

Inspector Combridge was a man who lived only for his profession. He honestly believed that it is one of the main purposes of the complex edifice of our civilization to detect and punish the breaches of law which may be committed among its members. No cajolery, however skilful, no bribery, however large, no consideration of pity, no respect for individual freedom, would have power to deflect him for a single inch from the path of duty, as he saw it. If he himself were guilty of lie or fraud, it was always and only that he might bring the criminal whom he was pursuing to his legally destined end.

But the integrity of Inspector Combridge did not prevent him from being somewhat subconsciously influenced by the charming personality of Miss Evelyn Merivale, and it was with a voice and manner which contrasted with his usual attitude in receiving those whom he invited to such interviews that he had shaken hands and welcomed his expected visitor.

"You are Miss Evelyn Merivale," he commenced, with a formal politeness, "of Saxton Hall?"

Miss Merivale allowed herself a slight expression of surprise as she answered, "I used to live there."

"You are the only daughter of Sir James Saxton?"

"I don't see what that has to do with—"

"No," interrupted the Inspector, with one of those swift counters in which he rarely allowed himself to exhibit his mental alertness. "You want to see me about a dog."

"I don't want to see you at all," she answered, with a lightness of tone that discounted the rudeness of the return.

"Yet you may be saving much trouble to yourself and others. If I am correctly informed, you have been acting as secretary to Lady Barbara Dillington for about five months past?"

"Would you kindly tell me who has been giving you information which concerns no one but myself?"

"There is no difficulty about that. Lady Barbara always engages her staff through the same agency. Will you please tell me something which I do not know? How did you first become acquainted with Mr. Wilfrid Ralston?"

"He was of some assistance to me at a time of momentary difficulty when I first came to London."

"May I take it that that was your first acquaintance— when he was of indirect assistance to you in obtaining your present position, without disclosing the application to your own relatives—without, in fact, the references which the agency would normally require?"

"You seem to know everything. You may not be aware that he had himself no idea who I was at the time."

"But he met Lord Britleigh?"

"Only as—as Mr. Warden. As a man whom I was avoiding—whom he assisted me to elude." Something brought a smile to her lips as her thoughts went backward to her sudden flight from Saxton, and the abortive pursuit which followed.

"Do you mind telling me, Miss Merivale, why you are occupying your present position?"

"Does it matter to anyone but myself?"

"It is possible that it may. I should like to be clear as to Lord Britleigh's action in the matter. You have your own fortune?"

"I haven't a bean."

"Then Lord Britleigh cannot have been influenced by a wish to—to control your money?"

"No. Why should he, even if I'd got any? He's got piles."

"Yes," said the Inspector thoughtfully. "So he has. There's no doubt of that." He made a brief blotting-pad note. "Sir James Saxton's will." He resumed in a brisker tone.

"You are right, Miss Merivale, that this is not the subject on which I asked you to see us. But it happens that both Lord Britleigh and Mr. Ralston are concerned—of course, in very different ways—in the recent incidents it is my duty to probe, and—well, you never know what may help. It's a small world to those of us who watch it from this angle of Scotland Yard. I understand that you allowed Mr. Ralston to use Belleville Gardens as an accommodation address?"

"Yes. I did."

"It was scarcely wise?"

"It was a silly thing to do."

"An act of business, may I ask, or of friendship only?"

"Friendship, of course."

"And you went alone to see him at River Street at about 2:00 A.M. on the morning of the 23rd instant? May I call that a sillier thing still?"

"Yes, you may if you like; but I'm not sure. It didn't turn out as it should, but I think it was the right thing to do."

"It was extremely foolish; will you tell me what induced you to visit him at that time and place?"

"I went to warn him that he was dealing with people that were not fit to be trusted."

"May I ask how you learnt that?"

"I don't mind telling you anything that I did myself, but I'm not going to give other people away."

"You must please look at matters rather differently from that, Miss Merivale. Your first duty is to the State of which you are a citizen, and to give such information as may be required without reference to whom it may affect, whether for good or evil. Only I ought to say that you are not bound to say anything which would incriminate yourself."

"I don't look at things quite like that."

"Well, you must please try. Was it Lord Britleigh?"

"If you know everything, I don't see why you need to ask."

"Very well. Do you mean me to understand that Lord Britleigh warned you that his co-directors were planning to cheat Mr. Ralston of the fruits of his invention, or that his personal safety was in jeopardy?"

"I don't mean you to understand either. It was nothing he said. It was an impression which I gained."

"You mean that he did not intend that anything he said should lead to Mr. Ralston being warned, and he left you without knowing of your intention?"

"Yes. I've no doubt he did."

"Are you certain that whatever threat was implied was directed against Mr. Wilfrid and not against Mr. Dudley Ralston?"

"Yes. I regarded Mr. Dudley as one of the dangers himself."

"Will you tell me just what happened after your arrival in River Street? I may tell you this first, Miss Merivale. You were seen to enter and leave, and the number of your car was taken. I have Mr. Ralston's account, and so far what you have told me tends to confirm it in some unessential particulars. If you can give an independent account of what happened within the house which confirms it further you may be doing him a very good turn indeed. I don't know that you have any reason to wish to do that, but I suppose that any of us would save an innocent man from the gallows if the occasion should arise."

"I don't know quite where you want me to begin. You know I went alone in the car. It wasn't quite as late as you think. I was back in the garage at 2:27. I noticed the clock there. It must have been about twenty to two when I got to River Street. I found the place quickly enough, because Wilfrid had described it to me, in case I ever had occasion to go. It was freezing hard in the street, and it was quite dark there, apart from the lamps, but it was too dark in the entry to see even the wall, and it was muddy at the top and near the door. I stepped into a puddle there, and one foot got soaked."

"Yes. I know that. We've had a cast of your shoe since last Thursday morning."

"It seems waste of time telling you anything. I knocked at the door two or three times before I felt where the push was, and then I rang, and Wilfrid came to the door. Then we went upstairs, and...." the girl paused, as though reluctant to carry the narrative into further detail, "we went into a room upstairs. Perhaps you know that too."

"Not the laboratory?"

"No. It couldn't have been. t was a kind of living-room in a mess."

"Was anyone else there?"

"No. No one at all. Wilfrid said we were alone in the house. It was afterwards that he said that."

"After?"

"After I'd told him what I had heard, and he'd thanked me for it."

"Then I wanted to go. And he asked me to marry him, as he was always doing. And I told him that I never should. And he said that he shouldn't take that. And I got angry and made it plainer than I had done before. And he said then I shouldn't have come there, and he'd see that I talked differently before I left. And then I tried to push past him, and he tried to lock the door, and I struck him on the side of the face, and got out of the room."

"Yes," said the Inspector, "I noticed the bruise."

"There wasn't much light on the landing," she went on, "and I must have got to the head of the wrong stairs by when he followed me out and switched on a landing light. He called to me that I couldn't get out that way. I think he'd got calmer then, and wouldn't have made any more trouble, but I wasn't sure, and when he came to the head of the stairs I started down. And then he gave an exclamation. I think it was 'What in hell's that?' It was in a very startled voice, and I looked down—it was almost dark at the foot of the stairs, where they curved sideways to the hall—and I thought I saw that the banisters were broken away, and there was something black lying there, and I've not been sure since whether it was his voice that frightened me or what I saw, but I turned, and he pushed past me down the stairs, and I ran back across the landing, and down the stairs that I ought to have taken at first.

"I found the door, though there was hardly any light. I think I ran straight to it. But when I got to it, it was locked, and I couldn't get it opened at first, and I heard him call to me as though he was more frightened than before. It was 'Evelyn, don't go,' or 'Evelyn, come here,' but I got the door open then, and I'd had enough of that house. There's nothing more, except that the engine wouldn't start at first—it had got cold—and I thought he'd come out before I could get away."

"You couldn't swear to what you saw at the foot of the stairs?"

"I didn't know what it was then. Of course, I do now."

"You didn't guess?"

"No. I don't think I did. But Wilfrid had upset me before that, and it's hard to say which it was that made me so anxious to get away."

"And there's nothing more to tell?"

"No. I don't think so."

"You weren't hurt at all?"

"Not in the least."

"But your dress was less fortunate?"

"How—?"

"They noticed it at the garage when you took the car in."

"You don't miss much," she said in genuine admiration.

"We try not to miss anything. You won't wear that dress again? Bill, at the garage, says it was torn to the waist."

"Then Bill used his imagination more than his eyes. It wasn't torn to—well, anyway, I'd mended it before I went to bed when I got back, and I've worn it twice since."

"And now, Miss Merivale," the Inspector said in his more official voice, "I'm just going to ask you to sign a statement setting out the facts as you've told them to me, and after that I sincerely hope that we shan't need to trouble you again. You've been of great help to us, and though you must have had a very unpleasant experience, you'll have the satisfaction of thinking that you've helped to clear suspicion from an innocent man, and turn our attention into the right direction. I may tell you that your account agrees with that of Mr. Ralston in all essential particulars, and they are both consistent with that which we have obtained from another man who was there earlier in the evening, though I'm not saying that it shows that he's telling the truth. Pass me those sheets, Fordyce, if you've got them ready."

112

Miss Merivale found herself gazing upon six sheets of foolscap paper written in a very neat and rapid hand, and purporting to be the account which she had just given.

It commenced, "I, Evelyn Merivale...having been duly cautioned," etc.

"Have I?" she said, smiling.

"Well, if not, I will now. You are under no obligation to sign this statement, which is a voluntary one on your part, and anything which it contains may be used in evidence.... Of course, it's a mere formality in this instance."

Evelyn glanced over the sheets rapidly. She admired the skill of the condensation and the absence of corrections, and was half annoyed and half amused at the curious jargon into which her words had been changed. She saw the absurdity of anyone "voluntarily" making a statement that he had been "duly cautioned." Why should he? That was inserted by the police to protect themselves. She had a vague realization of the necessary defects of these hybrid documents which are neither a straightforward record of examination, nor an original statement, but she was not greatly concerned. Also, she was in a hurry to go. She would already have to do some further lying to explain the length of her absence. Must she resurrect that dog; and how would it avail her now? She signed and initialled as quickly as possible at the various positions indicated.

CHAPTER XX.

DETECTIVE ISAACS quickened his pace as he saw that Inspector Combridge was in the act of entering his waiting car. He waved a fat hand to the chauffeur, who paused for the moment necessary for him to gain the door.

"I've got him, sir," he said breathlessly. It did his heart no good to have to hurry like that.

"Got Ringbolt? Where is he?"

"He isn't arrested yet, but he's where he can't get away."

"There's no such place, Isaacs, when we're dealing with a man like that. Not if he's got friends. I told you if you once got on his track to run him in, warrant or no warrant. We'd soon have got him to talk when he began to feel a pain in his neck." The Inspector was out of the car now. The appointment must wait. "Come and tell me just what you have found." He led the way back to his office.

Isaacs had recovered his breath, though he was still sensible of the injustice of the rebuke he had received when he had not been in a condition to refute it adequately. Standing before the Inspector's desk, he pulled out his notebook, and read his report:

"Elijah Ringbolt, *alias* Stevens, *alias*...."

"Never mind that," said the Inspector sharply; you're not giving evidence now."

"...shipped as a stoker on the *Anaconda* at the Royal Albert Docks on the 21st instant under the name of James Stevens."

"Sure it's he?"

"Yes, sir. There's no doubt of that. The *Anaconda*'s due at Lisbon this afternoon. Shall I cable to have him detained?"

"Lisbon? I don't know that we could. Better just cable them to watch that he doesn't leave the ship, and keep him in sight if he does. Where does it call next? But the 21st? You must be wrong about that. That was two days before the murder."

"Yes, sir. But there's no doubt at all."

"I see. Well, you've done your part. If you're right, there's an end to that. It's as well to know. We don't want a false scent."

There was nothing more to be said. He had felt almost sure that if that man could be found. He was a man known to the police of four continents, in three of which he had suffered imprisonment for crimes of violence and robbery. He had been held for nearly a year at Mozambique for a particularly brutal murder, and finally released for lack of evidence. This man had been seen hanging about River Street by P.C. 626H more than once within a fortnight of the murder. He had once seen him enter the passage that led to the back of the house, and had fetched him out with a warning. Mrs. Belinda Miggs had observed him also, and had given a very accurate description of some unattractive physical features. The Inspector had not doubted that if he could lay this man by the heels he would have secured the actual assassin. He thought it likely that he was a tool in the hands of others, and that his confession would draw such fish to the Inspector's net as would place his own name high on the records of Scotland Yard. That he had not been seen in his usual haunts since the search had started was only a further confirmation of the suspicion against him.

"Well," he said again, "if you're sure.... So that's that." He went back to his waiting car more determined than before that he would not be defeated at the appointment he had made.

"I want the Head Office of the London and Northern. It's just beyond King Street, on the right. I've got an appointment there for eleven with Sir Reginald Crowe. You'd better slip along. It's nearly that now."

The car slid smoothly into the stream of traffic, and the Inspector settled his mind to face the unexpected rebuff it had received.

CHAPTER XXI.

"I THOUGHT it best to see you yourself, Sir Reginald, rather than make a written protest. Your general manager has—"

"Yes, I know. He acted on my instructions."

"It isn't often that we meet with a refusal in a matter of this—"

"Well, you've met one now." The tone made the words less offensive than they would otherwise have been. The Inspector saw amusement rather than any more aggressive quality in the eyes that met his, but he was not mistaken in the difficulty of the task he had undertaken. He knew the reputation of the man he approached—a man slim and muscular, alert both of mind and body, and looking very young for the position he occupied—that of Chairman of one of the largest and most enterprising of the London banks.

As though reading his thoughts, Sir Reginald asked, "Do you know why I am sitting here now? If I tell you that, you won't be surprised that you didn't get the information you wanted."

Inspector Combridge knew a good deal, but it was a knowledge which he usually preferred to keep in his own mind. He indicated politely that he would like to know Sir Reginald's account of the matter.

"Well, it's soon told. Do you know what's an Englishman's worse fault?"

"No," said the Inspector, admitting ignorance with more than his usual sincerity. "You've got me there. I can't say that I do."

"Well, it's always thinking that the weather won't change; and the only sure thing about it is that it always does. If the sun's shining today he says, 'What about going on the river on Wednesday week?' If it's pouring rain he says, 'I'd get up a picnic this day month if the weather wasn't so bad.'

"It's the same in business and everything else. When we had the cotton boom up North folk didn't say, 'We're going to have a good year's trade.' They went on floating companies at silly figures, as though there'd never be any change to the world's end.

"Well, I made a bit in the swim, and then turned round and sold, and went on selling. I'd sell any shares on the list for a forward date at something under the market price, and I lost that I'd made while the boom held, and then when the slump began I just raked it in.

"It was about that time that a bit of information leaked out that cost me a hundred thousand, more or less, and I didn't rest till I found out how. It was my bank manager, who'd been blabbing at lunch.

"So I made a row with the bank, and said if they'd sack the fool I'd sit back, but if they wouldn't I'd make them pay. When they wouldn't do that I brought an action. I was too young to know then that a man had better lose his left ear than let the lawyers get their hands in his pockets. So I lost the case and appealed, and got an order for a new trial, and lost that, and appealed again, and was signing cheques all the time, and getting madder every day. And then I tried a new plan. I knew the bank couldn't be doing well, with the slump there was, and half their business up North being done in the cotton trade. I raised every shilling I could, and then began selling their shares. It took six months to finish that fight, but it's soon told now. The market wavered at first, and then steadied, and sell as I would there were always those who would buy. But the market broke in the end, and I got home. It was only just in time. When we took stock we found that the public had got frightened at last and had sold out. The shares were all held by operators, or by myself, or the directors of the bank, and the aces were in my hand.

"There came a day when I met the Board, and three out of four of them ruined men if I drew in the line, for they'd bought up to the last. You see, they knew that the position was sound enough, and their only fear had been at the first that there'd be a run on the bank if the shares broke too much.

"So they asked what I meant to do, and I told them that I meant to be Chairman of that board, and to hold enough stock to make sure that I should stay where I am now, and beyond that they could run loose. And I said that those who had skinned themselves out to back the bank could keep their seats on the Board, and have their shares back at the right price, but the rest could quit—and there was a bank manager to be sacked, if they didn't mind.

"Now, since I've sat here I've let everyone on our staff know that I might forgive anything else, even if they got their hand in the till at the wrong time, but a blabber will always quit. And after I've told you that, have you still got the nerve to ask me for the lady's name?"

"Oh, yes," said the Inspector cheerfully. He had listened patiently to an account which he already knew, though it had been told him from another angle, but he considered that a man is usually in a good humour when he has told such an anecdote, and he was conscious that he would need the assistance of every favourable circumstance if he were to succeed in the object he had in mind. "Oh, yes," he said, "because I'm not asking for the same thing at all. I'm not asking you to give any information about the lady. I'll find that out for myself. And I'm not inquiring for her as a customer, whether she be one or not, but simply as one who presented a cheque in error which you quite properly declined to pay."

"I'm sorry, Inspector Combridge, but I can only give you the same reply."

The Inspector decided to lay his cards on the table with an unusual freedom. It may have appeared to him that a banker who felt so strongly on the etiquette of reticence should be capable of treating the information confidentially. He said, "Will you at least listen for a few minutes while I explain the reason for which I ask?"

"Yes," Sir Reginald answered dubiously, "I won't refuse to listen, if you'll make it short. But I've got a lot to get through before lunch."

"I'll be as short as I can. You've heard, of course, of the Bell Street murder, and you know there's been no arrest. It took place in a half-empty house that wasn't regularly occupied. You've probably read about that in the Press, but there's a lot that you won't have heard, because we haven't let it come out. There was a room let to a Mr. Wilfrid Ralston, the brother of the murdered man, where he's been experimenting with an invention that they think is worth a large sum. I don't know whether it really is, but there's no doubt that they thought it was.

"There's talk of a million pounds. And, for some reason, till it gets patented it's a secret that isn't easy to keep.

"On the day of the murder the position was that Wilfrid Ralston was trying to sell to Vantons, Ltd., Dudley Ralston was trying to steal the secret of the invention, and one at least of the directors of Vantons was in touch with Dudley with the object of purchasing at an advantage if he were successful in stealing it.

"You'd say at once—anyone would—that if Dudley got murdered it wouldn't be much more than he deserved, and that it would be something to do with that secret, whether he'd succeeded in stealing it or not, and that a quarrel between the two brothers would be the most likely explanation. That's a fact, and it's another that the two brothers were there that night, and the director of Vantons as well—"

"Not Britleigh?"

"No."

"It wouldn't be him. Nichols?"

"That's a good guess. Professor Blinkwell'd been there as well, but he was invited to do so. He doesn't really come into the count."

"I wouldn't trust Blinkwell too far."

"Nor would I. But he's not the sort to throw a bigger man down the stairs, and then cut his head off."

"Probably not. You can let Blinkwell go."

"In any case, he wasn't there. I've checked that."

"Very well. What's the trouble? Can't you get the salt on the right tail?"

"I'm not trying. I don't say I'm sure, but I don't think the murder was anything to do with Wilfrid Ralston's invention at all. I could tell better if I could find out how Dudley lived, and you've got the only clue in your own hands."

"That doesn't sound sense. There must be a hundred ways of finding out how he spent his time."

"So there are, but the question is how he made about £26,000 in the last two years, and there's no answer to that."

"Cards?"

"I can't find that he ever played high. He wasn't a man of overmuch courage or big ideas."

"Well, what's yours?"

Sir Reginald was interested, but he had other things on his mind. He looked pointedly at his watch.

"My idea? I've got three that'll fit the facts; but it's the illicit drug trade that seems the most likely."

"What's your reason for thinking that?"

"Oh, we think of it all the time. There's an organization that we cannot reach, and we're all on the watch, here and in New York, and Paris, and Berlin, and half the ports in the world."

"Well, you ought to know better than I. I've no doubt the profits are big enough, but I can't see a man selling to make £10,000 a year without something that you could find when you're once looking his way."

"Nor can I, if he peddled it out. But that's not my idea. You know, the real trouble in this trade is to get the stuff through the customs without being seized. Of course, they can't declare it for what it is. Every now and then we seize a parcel—we had about £40,000 worth at Marseilles about a month ago, but they just let it go, and I suppose the profits are too big for them to mind. That was a mixed lot—heroin, morphine, and cocaine. The whole lot wouldn't weigh a couple of tons, and a lot of that would be the soldered cases in which it was packed. They'd probably have netted about £200,000 the way they'd have sold that lot if they once got it out East.

"We keep a good lookout, but we can't examine every cargo on every wharf in the world. We can't broach every cask, and open every bale, and the way they do is to pass it about till it sails from a port where no one would guess it to be. It may go from Hull to Stockholm for a start, and then to heaven knows where, and then when it's well lost it comes in to its destination from some unlikely place, and gets passed along while they're holding up two or three other suspicious cargoes that turn out to be on the square.

"Now, one of the troubles of getting it through in this way is that it's got to be kept somewhere after it's unloaded till it gets shipped again, and it can't be in the hands of those who control the trade, for they won't run any risk of getting jailed. They're too high up, and even at the Yard we can't find out who they are. It might be the

Commissioner himself, or it might be you, for all we know, if you don't mind me putting it in that way."

"Not at all. It's an idea. Go ahead."

"Well, if you or I'd got to pick a man to take charge of a little lot of that kind, what sort should we be likely to pick? I figure it this way—we couldn't expect a saint, but we'd want a man we could trust not to clear off with it if he got the chance, knowing that we couldn't squeal, and one who wouldn't blab, and that means one who didn't drink overmuch. A man like that would have to be well paid, and it would be best to have one whose ideas weren't too big. One who'd feel that the fee we paid was a very big thing, and if he was of a rather timid kind, so much the better. And, of course, he'd have to be one with a clean bill. One that wasn't under notice of the police.

"That's how it seems to me, and when I sum Dudley Ralston up, it's just about what he was. But it doesn't follow that he hadn't tried to double-cross them, whoever they are, or he might simply have felt that he'd made enough, and wouldn't stand for the risk again."

"And you think he was murdered by the gang? Would they go to such lengths as that?"

"Yes, of course. With such sums at stake, and with the class of men that they have to trust, they're almost bound to have a death now and then. It's the only discipline that they have.

"You can see that in the States, by the way the bootleggers are getting to use their guns. It's the only way they have of keeping their own accounts square."

"Is this just a guess, or have you got something to go on, beyond that?"

"I thought I had till half an hour before I came here. We'd got evidence of a man who'd been hanging round, who'd have killed his own child for a pint of gin, and we thought I'd only got to catch him, and I might learn a lot, but I've just learnt that I've been barking under the wrong tree. The man sailed on an outgoing boat two days before the murder was done."

"There's nothing beyond that? You found no evidence in the house?"

"No. Nothing at all."

"Then it's a very thin guess."

"I don't say you're wrong. But the trouble is to get anything else that will fit the facts equally well."

Inspector Combridge did not conceal that he was a worried man. He had felt himself that it sounded like a "thin guess" as he had set it out. It still seemed a probability in his own mind, but he recognized that when he put it into words it sounded—thin.

Sir Reginald sat for a short moment in thoughtful silence. Then he gave his decision. "I'm not going to refuse to help you. I know Britleigh. We've been in some things together, and we're in one or two now. I'll have a straight talk with him, and after that I'll have my own idea as to where Vantons stand.

"I'll do more than that. If you promise to leave my cashiers alone, I'll find out who the lady is for myself, and I'll go over her own account. I'll find out more about her and those she's in with in half a day than your men could get at in a week, and some things, perhaps, that you'd never get at all if you subpoenaed two-thirds of the staff. If I'm satisfied, I'll tell you, and you'll know that you've been saved from wasted time, and if I'm not we'll have another talk."

Sir Reginald rose quickly with the last word, and led the Inspector to the door without exacting the promise for which he had stipulated. Perhaps he relied upon the Inspector's good sense to know when he was well off.

The Inspector left the Bank premises in better spirits than he had entered them. People differed about the character of Sir Reginald Crowe, but it would have been admitted equally by friends and foes that when he took a thing up he had a habit of seeing it through.

He had only just left the building when there came an urgent inquiry from Scotland Yard, asking whether he were still there. He was sitting in his car in Fleet Street in a traffic block when his eyes were attracted by the placards of the evening papers at the street corner:

ANOTHER BELL STREET MURDER!

SECOND MURDER IN HOXTON!

Half a minute later a passing constable had been instructed to ring up Scotland Yard with a message to say that he was on his way to Bell Street, and his car had disappeared in that direction at a pace which took little heed of the traffic regulations or the safety of the crowded streets.

CHAPTER XXII.

"COMBRIDGE, said the Assistant Commissioner, "I don't want to be unfair, but it seems to me that you've got us into a very nasty mess."

"Yes, sir," said the Inspector.

The frankness of this admission and the silence that followed seemed to act as a further irritant to Sir Henry Clobson. He burst out in a more evident anger. "What's the use of standing there, and saying 'Yes, sir,' to everything? I've told you that you've got us into a hell of a mess, and I don't want to know that you think the same. It doesn't matter what you think. What I want to hear is how you're going to get us out. How do you think it's going to sound at the inquest that a man gets murdered, and we can't find anything out for ourselves, so we tell his innocent brother that unless he finds it out for us we'll lock him up for the crime that he's as innocent of as you or me, and so he takes on our job, and gets murdered as well, and we still knowing no more about it than an unborn babe? I'll tell you what, Combridge, if you don't get this dished up differently before the inquest opens there'll be some resignations to sign, and I don't mean mine to be the only one, if it's got to go in."

"Yes, sir," said the Inspector. "I don't see that it need come out quite like that."

"Don't you? Then I'd like to know how you think it will, with this Jelly-paste or Jelly-puddle, or whatever he is, sitting there to watch the interests of the murdered man. Didn't he tell you that he was doing it all on his lawyer's advice? Do you suppose *he* doesn't know?"

"It was really on Mr. Ralston's own suggestion," said the Inspector mildly.

"And much good that'll do us, even if it's believed. If that's all you've got to say."

"I don't think Mr. Jellipot looks at it quite as you put it, sir. He's to be here in half an hour."

"Anything else?" asked Sir Henry in a slightly mollified voice, his habitual confidence in the Inspector's ability making a faint effort to assert itself. "I don't mean that nonsense about 'Watch them.' I don't want to hear that again. Watch who, I should like to know? Watch the stable-door when the horse is in the next county?"

"I don't think that was quite what it meant, sir. I think the 'M' was separate."

"Very well. Have it your own way. Watch the 'm.' Much sense in that! I should like to know how you'll begin. Watch the milk, I suppose, as that was the fluid used. Yes, if you've nothing more to report. You can go home and watch the milk. If you hadn't let Crowe bluff you over that cheque, you might have had something."

"Sir Reginald has telephoned from Pontefract, sir. He said he would be here by nine-thirty tonight. He's coming by road."

"Then he couldn't do it in the time."

"I told him the speed limit ˚didn't apply in this instance."

"And what help will he be?"

"He seems to think that he can help us a good deal. It mayn't turn out quite as you fear, sir. Though it's too early to say."

"I'm sorry if I've been a bit hasty, Combridge, but you can guess how I feel. Anything else?"

"Miss Merivale will be here in a few minutes. I have sent the fast car."

"Sent the.... You don't mean to add another Savidge case to the trouble we've got already? We've got no...."

"I don't think Miss Merivale will make any difficulty. She seemed quite willing to come here. She's more concerned about when she gets back. I undertook to do the explaining to Lady Barbara."

"Anything else?"

"Only that if you won't need me for the next few minutes I should be glad to get some tea while I can."

"Very well. Yes, of course. You must need something by now. You've had a hard time since last night. I'm sorry I kept you standing there. You mustn't take all I've said too seriously."

"No, sir. I'll go now, if you don't mind." He left the room before Sir Henry could think of anything else with which to hinder him. It had been an interview, to his thinking, of very useless words.

CHAPTER XXIII.

THE Inspector sat in his own room, a quarter of an hour later, with Miss Merivale and Mr. Jellipot, whom he had introduced to each other, and whom he proposed to take into a common confidence.

"I think it's due to you, Mr. Jellipot, as Mr. Wilfrid Ralston's legal adviser, that I should explain without reservations how the present position has arisen; and as I understand that he had instructed you to refer to Miss Merivale on at least one important matter in case he should meet with any—serious accident, I thought it might save time if she were here too, and I'm sure you'll both pardon me if I go over anything that either of you know, but the other mayn't.

"When I saw him last Monday I told him that he wasn't free from suspicion, but I didn't go beyond that, and I let him see plainly enough that I didn't think he was guilty, but I thought that if it were known that he were detained here on suspicion it might help us in getting on the right track. Well, he didn't like it, and you couldn't expect he would, but I think I could have persuaded him to consent—I wish I had, for his own sake now—if he hadn't put forward another suggestion that seemed too good to be turned down.

"He said that he was spending most of the daytime at his laboratory in Bell Street, and that Professor Blinkwell was with him most of the time, and that he was preparing

129

the demonstration on the success of which the sale of his patent would depend. He told me that if he had a few hours more to complete the work he was doing he could erect a screen which would retain a record of everything that went on in that room unless it were in absolute darkness. He was preparing this in collaboration with Professor Blinkwell, and he believed he could trust him, but he wasn't really doing so altogether. Rather, he was going a way that would prove whether he were fit to trust. He was preparing his material so that it would provide the demonstration, but it was really commercially useless in the form in which he was making it, because *it wouldn't last more than a short time*. I didn't learn how long. He may have meant a few days or a few hours. I wished I'd asked more exactly now. But I suppose it's something like having a negative that isn't fixed—the picture is there, but it fades away. Anyway, the position was so that if they were on the square he'd give them the right formula, and everything would be all right all round, but if they tried any tricks, they'd find they'd got a dud thing when they'd shown their hand and it was too late to pretend they'd meant a straight deal.

"I asked him if he wasn't afraid that if he gave away so much they'd find out the rest for themselves, but he said that the chances against it being worked out were about 200,000 to one, even if they knew the thing that was missing.

"He said that he'd only got it by working backward, so to speak—that it was only after he'd found out the surface that *does* retain the picture that he found out that a simpler or incomplete preparation would take it, but so that it soon faded away. That's the best I can explain, and how much can be saved, or what's gone with him, you may know better than I.

"But the point is now that it seemed a good thing to me that he should go on with his own plan. He was to finish the screen, with the Professor's help, and he told me that he meant to leave some of the material lying about in the room, and if anyone came and took it away, it wouldn't be any use to them, but he'd have a record on the screen, and know just what had occurred. It seemed to me that anyone who would be likely to attempt that would see their danger for themselves, but I suppose that if that deterred them it wouldn't be any harm to him. He was right enough either way with the fake material he was using, if that isn't an unfair word. But if there were any attempt to get into the house for other purposes—say for something that is thought to be hidden there—they wouldn't be likely to guess that the screen would give them away, and we might have a record that would tell us just what we want to know.

"Now, you've heard how it's turned out. He finished the screen as he had planned, and set it up, and Professor Blinkwell left him there the night before last—the Professor says he always liked to stay behind at night, which is probable enough—but he said he didn't mean to be long, and the Professor went back yesterday morning, and rang in the way they had agreed, and got no answer, and thought he was late coming, and went away. But he says he had an uneasy feeling, knowing all that was at stake in that room, and so he went back half an hour later, and getting no reply again he very properly reported it to the Hoxton Station, and they rang us up at the Yard and got instructions to break in at once, and I suppose you've heard what they found."

The Inspector paused at this point. He had the usual male idea that a woman cannot endure to hear of bloodshed or violence of any kind as well as a man, which is something less than a general truth, and he assumed (with good reason enough) that they had both read how Wilfrid Ralston had been found, lying dead with bullet wounds in body and head; but he resumed after a moment, with a realization that there were circumstances that must be told if he were to make his point clear.

"Of course, it's guess-work, more or less, but we think that what happened was this. The first shot came from behind, and struck him in the back of the skull, rather on the left. It struck at an angle, going away, so to speak, though it sank into the bone, and its effect was that he collapsed as though he were dead. The man who fired the shot probably thought that he was, but he fired into his body as he lay, to make extra sure.

"After a time, when the murderer must have gone, he came to himself, and found he was bleeding to death from the second bullet, which had missed the heart and gone through the lungs.

"He wasn't one to give up while there was a chance left, and he made an effort to get something to staunch the wound. He crawled some yards to the table, and pulled a cloth down that was on it, with all the litter that the table held. Among this was a bottle of milk, which fell on its side, and spilled over the floor.

"He gave up the attempt to stop the bleeding, which must have got worse as he moved, and he tried to write a message in milk on the floor, which was unfinished when he died. It must have been something that he felt to be very important for us to know, either for our own safety, or to secure his invention, or to bring his murderer to justice. We're not all agreed as to the details. Some of us think there was a struggle, and the cloth was pulled off then, and there's just a question as to which bullet was fired first, but I've told it you in the way that seems most likely to me. Now, I've got a photograph of what he tried to write, and here it is."

The Inspector handed them a blurred and straggling imitation of the words "WATCH THEM," but the last letter was somewhat farther apart than the three that preceded it, so that it did not require much imagination to suppose that the "M" was the commencement of a separate word, and this impression was supported by the smudge which followed, as though a useless effort had been made to complete the word with a failing hand.

"I don't know," he went on, "that I can reasonably expect you to give me much help in interpreting that riddle, but you are the only two who appear to have had the confidence of the murdered man, and if there is any warning he had given—any fear that he had expressed—any document that might help—"

"It is not a question," Mr. Jellipot replied, with precision, "to which you can expect an immediate and final negative, even though I am at a loss to make any helpful suggestion. It is one that requires reflection, and, perhaps, research among the documents which are in my possession. In the meantime, I would deprecate any relaxation of effort in other directions in the expectation that I should be able to render ultimate assistance. But there is another matter which appears to me to be of even greater importance, if not of an equal urgency.

"You tell me that in the demonstration which Mr. Ralston was preparing he was making use of a material which is of no assistance in securing the formula of his invention. In this particular he had been more frank with you than with me, possibly because he doubted whether I should approve of what was, after all, an attempt to secure his contract by a delusive proof, under whatever justification or provocation he may have resorted to that subterfuge.

"The matter which appears to me to be of the greatest importance is to ascertain whether the formula has perished with its inventor, and I confess I have but one hope for its recovery, and that is that Miss Merivale may be able to supply it.

"The matter of the greatest urgency, if I may say so, is not the studying of a writing the incompleteness of which renders it almost certainly indecipherable, but the interpretation, if it be by any means possible, of the screen which, you tell me, contains the fading picture of the scene of the tragedy—and we know not of what beside."

"But there is the possibility," the Inspector replied, "that the one may be the key—perhaps the only possible key—to the other."

"Yes," the lawyer admitted, "it is a possibility, but if it be one that we cannot turn? If it be no more than a broken key? Have you any idea of how long the screen will retain the impression which it receives?"

"None at all, beyond the fact that he used the word 'short,' and that it must have been sufficiently long to give him confidence that it would not fade before he had completed his demonstration, not only to the satisfaction of Professor Blinkwell, but of the whole Board of Vantons, who were to attend for that purpose."

"Then we seem to have at least two or three days, and probably more."

"Yes," the Inspector agreed. "So far as that goes, I've no doubt we have. But I've got the inquest to consider, and I think you'll agree, Mr. Jellipot, that we ought to have something to offer the jury—and the public—rather different from what we've got now. But Miss Merivale hasn't said anything yet?"

Evelyn had been content to wait till there should be a moment's interval in the remarks of the more talkative sex, as a sensible woman usually does under such circumstances. "Now," she said, "I can relieve your mind about one thing at once, Mr. Jellipot. I've got the formula with me now, and I left another copy at home. But they wouldn't either of them be worth sixpence except to one who knew how to read them. And I want to talk over that with you as soon as the Inspector's done with us both, because I think they ought to be secured differently. If I were to die at this moment it seems to me that Mr. Ralston's invention would be as utterly gone as though it hadn't been discovered at all, and with murder getting quite habit...."

"You can be sure that every precaution for your safety, Miss Merivale...," began the Inspector.

"Yes," she said cheerfully, "I'm not growing grey over that. But we'll have it safe, all the same. It isn't that the money can matter much now."

"There is a will," Mr. Jellipot interjected.

"Yes, I dare say. And there's a mother at Todmorden. But I expect she's too old for a million pounds to do much except bother her, as it would most people for that matter. But what I do think is that an invention of this importance ought to go to the credit of the man who discovered it. I think we ought to see that it isn't lost, and that...."

"We might call it 'Ralstonite'," Mr. Jellipot interjected again.

"...he gets the credit of what he has done. But about the writing, I'm inclined to think the 'm' was the beginning of a new word, though we can't do more than guess. It was the last letter he was able to write, and it wasn't a time when he'd be likely to space his words well enough to please a schoolmistress."

"It's the only chance that it'll tell us anything, anyway," Inspector Combridge agreed. "'Watch them' can't be any use to us. But it's not much better the other way. I thought at first it might be something in the room, and I gave orders that they weren't to move a thing, not even the litter from the floor. But when I sat in that room for half an hour I saw that it was no use.

"What can be the use of watching things that don't move? And there was scarcely anything that begins with 'm' in the whole room, except the milk itself. I thought of 'Watch the milk boil,' and wondered if it could be that, till I couldn't get it out of my head. When I tried to think of other words beginning with 'm' I couldn't get anything but that silly phrase 'Watch the milk boil,' till I began to fancy it was a telephonic message from the dead man, and gave it up, lest I should become sillier than I naturally am."

"I wouldn't dismiss it quite in that way," Mr. Jellipot said doubtfully. "Wasn't it rather singular that a bottle of milk should have been there at all?"

"No," Evelyn said; "milk is an ingredient in the composition."

"Doesn't that make it more likely that that was the word that he tried to write?"

"Perhaps it may, but, if so, it's nothing to do with the composition of the proper article. He told me it didn't matter how they were mixed. The composition sets itself at any ordinary temperature. He doesn't use heat at all."

"You'd be surprised how few things there are that begin with 'm' in that room," the Inspector continued. "I looked round at the floor and ceiling and walls, and the table and chairs, and an old gas-bracket, and first and last I got nothing but 'Watch the mat,' and what meaning is there in that?—thought of vague general words like the man or men, or the murderer, which were useless or silly, and I always got back at last to that wretched milk, till I gave it up for the time, and came away."

"Perhaps," Mr. Jellipot suggested, "a dictionary might—"

"I've got three of my best men on three different dictionaries now."

"It seems to me," Evelyn remarked, "the first thing to do is to try and read the screen. Mr. Ralston must have had a way in his mind, and it mayn't be as hard as we think. Suppose it's there that the clue lies? I mean, when we've seen what the screen shows we may be able to guess better what he was trying to warn us about."

"Then," said the Inspector, "perhaps you'll come with me at once. The car's waiting outside, and if there's anything more to be said we shall have time on the way."

"I'm afraid I can't come now," Mr. Jellipot replied; "I'm already late for an appointment with Samuels."

"I understand," the Inspector answered, "that Vantons claim that the agreement still stands? I rather thought that a man's death cancelled a personal document of that kind. Is that what they want to see you about now?"

Mr. Jellipot paused. He was not certain how far the legal position should be discussed, even in his present company.

"Not precisely," he said. "The present appointment was made before the news of Mr. Ralston's death came to my office. It concerns a question of stamping the document, on which Somerset House is asking a really absurd figure, and we were considering a modification of one of the clauses to get over the difficulty—a purely technical matter.

"Purely technical. It's not quite as simple as you think, Inspector. An agreement doesn't lapse as a matter of course. A good deal depends upon whether it's under seal. By the way, I had a talk with Mr. Levinstein this morning. He let out something that perhaps we ought to follow up. Perhaps 'let out' is hardly a fair expression to use. He seems a very shrewd man—a good business man, as his race usually are; but straight, as the best of them are, too. He seemed anxious to have matters handled in the right way, and having very little confidence that some of his colleagues had been working on those lines. That was the impression I got. But he told me that he was sure that Lord Britleigh and Wilfrid Ralston were old acquaintances. He didn't exactly imply anything against Lord Britleigh. I rather got the impression that he trusted him more than some of the rest, but it was just a fact that he thought you might like to know."

"I don't think there's anything in that," Evelyn interposed. "Nothing that I can't explain to the Inspector as we go along. It won't help us now."

So Mr. Jellipot went, and it was natural that the conversation turned to Lord Britleigh as soon as the two were seated in the car together.

"We'd better get anything said at once that you mightn't want Professor Blinkwell to hear," the Inspector began. "I've promised to pick him up at the Surrey Grill.... Talking about Lord Britleigh, do you mind telling me why you left home?"

Miss Merivale sat silent for a moment, and the Inspector waited for the snub which he had invited, but when she spoke she said simply, "I left home because my brother arranged my marriage without my consent, and I preferred to earn my own living."

"You will believe me, Miss Merivale, when I say that I am asking these questions from no idle curiosity. Would you tell me the name of the man who was suggested to you in this way?"

"It was Sir Reginald Crowe."

"And we may assume that it was a choice of which you did not approve?"

Evelyn answered this question with a very feminine indirectness. "I did not approve of any choice being made on my behalf."

The Inspector showed no sign that he had observed the implication of what wasn't said, as he hadn't voiced any expression of surprise when he heard Sir Reginald Crowe's name—and, after all, it was natural enough. He asked, "Did you ever learn the terms of your father's will?"

"I only know in a general way that Cyril inherited everything. I was very young when he died. I dare say you know that Cyril is sixteen years older than I. I don't think my father thought much of girls, anyway."

"Your father certainly showed great confidence in both your brother's integrity and ability. But the will was somewhat different from what you suppose. It is true that, till you marry, you are financially dependent upon your brother, but in that eventuality it becomes his obligation to pay you a third of the sum (apart from the value of the estates) which your father left. That is to say, a third of about £250,000."

"I've no doubt you are right, Inspector. It's such a habit with you. And it's very pleasant to hear. It would be still more exciting if I'd got anyone ready to go through the ceremony. But if you mean to suggest that Cyril's done away with the money, or something like that—well, it's the best joke I've heard since I left home. Cyril's got enough money to sink a ship."

"I didn't mean to suggest anything, Miss Merivale, that I didn't say. But if I did suggest, I should say this. Your brother is a very rich man. He has been very bold and successful in his financial ventures. They are the only real interest of his life. I think that he would feel about handing over £80,000 to you much as a chess-player would feel if he had to take off an important piece in the middle game. But Sir Reginald and he have been together in some of their bigger *coups*. I think what he meant to do was to arrange a marriage which would place your money where it would still be available for his financial adventures, and to secure the co-operation of Sir Reginald more closely than before."

"Yes," she said, "that's the kind of thing Cyril would try. He must have had the shock of his life when he came down to breakfast and I wasn't there."

She thought for some moments of those exciting days when he found where she was, and she had evaded him again with Wilfrid Ralston's help—never really taking Wilfrid into her confidence, so that he had continued to think of her brother by the name of Warden, in which he had registered at her hotel (anything to avoid publicity—just like Cyril again!), and had supposed him to be a pursuing suitor, rather than the brother that he really was.

Wilfrid had been devoted to her, in his own way. He had not got much in return. In fact, as she had known him better she had liked him less. It was an intimacy that he had forced from the first, though it had been very cleverly, very delicately done. But he had loved her all the same, in his own way; he had trusted her too, and she was resolved, if it lay in her power, he should have justice now.

"This is Professor Blinkwell, Miss Merivale," the Inspector was saying. The car, which had stopped for a moment at the kerb, moved on again.

CHAPTER XXIV.

PROFESSOR BLINKWELL observed Miss Merivale with as much attention as the laws of courtesy will permit, and Miss Merivale observed the Professor to equal purpose without looking at him at all. She came to the conclusion that he was a man of brains, and if he were willing to help he would be an ally worth having. Beyond that he had a personality that left her cold. She felt, and instinctively resented, his own attitude toward her, which may be described as one of scientific inquiry.

He was not promiscuously susceptible to women. He had a charming wife of his own, of whom he was very fond. In this case he was very ill-pleased to observe that the Inspector had a companion at all. He was as resolved as they could be to find out the secrets of that room of death, and he was intending to propose to the Inspector that they should both spend the night there for that purpose. Probably the Inspector would refuse (he had already been up all last night), and the ground would be left clear for himself, which he would very greatly prefer. He did not suppose that Miss Merivale would wish to stay all night; in any event, not if the Inspector should leave.

"I am not," he remarked to the Inspector, as the conversation quickly turned to the subject which was in all their minds, "primarily concerned in the commercial problems which will arise in consequence of this unfortunate— of this dreadful murder. But it seems to me that we are placed in a very difficult—it may be in a very invidious position. I feel the difficulty of my own position somewhat acutely. I am acting primarily for Vantons, Ltd. That is my duty, and my interest also. My first concern is to prove beyond doubt the commercial quality of this invention—of its originality, or that it could be the subject of a valid patent, there can be no doubt at all. But though I am acting, and must continue to act, in that capacity, I had also, as I think you know, been taken into Mr. Ralston's confidence a good deal during the last few days. We had worked together in the preparation of the composition of which his invention consists. With a degree of confidence which I have felt very much—at which I am deeply touched, and which I shall never forget—he has really placed his secret in my hands. My difficulty is that I had—or thought I had—detected at least one serious flaw—on one point I had already suggested alteration—in the process which he has used. There is nothing surprising in that—nothing which reflects upon the greatness of his discovery, or the credit which is due to him as its originator. The inventions are few indeed which are developed perfectly from their first inception.

"Had he lived I am sure that no difficulty would have arisen. I should not have wished to detract unfairly from the merit of his process as it had first been submitted for my examination. He, on his side, would, I am sure, have wished that just recognition should be given to any assistance, whether much or little, which I have been or may still be able to render. My difficulty is that I am now become the judge of my own case, and in such circumstances that no one will be in a position to question my decision."

The Inspector said only, "Yes. It's rather awkward for you." He was not sure how far he trusted Professor Blinkwell. It has been said that every man has his price. The price here was very high. But he remembered also that the Professor was mistaken in thinking that he had had so complete a confidence. Now, the transient nature of the screen's impression would probably be discovered—must be so, sooner or later, unless he or Mr. Jellipot should come forward to substitute the true formula for that which the Professor believed to be authentic, and of which he had doubtless a sufficient note already. And Wilfrid Ralston had made a solemn declaration on his agreement that no such written evidence existed. His death had certainly made more difficulty than that on which the Professor had remarked.

Evelyn cut the knot with what may have been a calculating indiscretion. She said, "I think I may be able to help you there, Professor. You know, I'm a sister of Lord Britleigh, and I was also a friend of Wilfrid Ralston, so I'm on both sides, so to speak. Mr. Ralston gave me some figures to keep in case a position arose such as we have to face now, and if they are no good, and you show that you have improved the process from what it was then, I think everyone would recognize what you have done."

The Professor gave no sign of feeling of any kind as he received that somewhat startling information. He said slowly, "That does alter matters a good deal. It alters them all round." He was not so sure that he was sorry that she had come.

Whatever Inspector Combridge thought of this confidence, he only said, "You can't wonder, Professor, that he took some extra precaution after his brother's death. It's turned out very fortunate that he did."

Evelyn remembered that the formula had been given to her while Dudley was still alive, but she said no more. She may have realized that she had been sufficiently indiscreet already.

She turned the conversation to the question of reading the secret that the screen must hold of what had happened last night in the room of death. But the Professor was not encouraging. He had no doubt that it was there. But there was no possible commencement by which it could be discovered, and by which it could be read. In a sense it was there, but it was beyond the possibility of human reach. What did he think of the writing in milk? Did he think there were only two words?

No. He thought the "M" was a separate letter. He had given it a good deal of thought, but he said frankly that he was baffled. A single letter was too faint a clue. He pointed out that the possibility was not only that of a noun. It might have been a verb; or even an adjective; which would define a noun to which they had no clue whatever. But he thought that the murderer would be captured, all the same. He remarked upon the extraordinary habit which murderers have of throwing weapons away in the neighbourhood of the crime, usually such as will inevitably direct suspicion in their directions. The Inspector agreed.

Evelyn said no more. Her mind still held to its pursuit of the letter "m." A provoking letter. Watch the mate? or the midshipman? The midden or the mulligatawny? Almost any letter would have been better than "m."

CHAPTER XXV.

"I DON'T see what more we can do here, Miss Merivale; not tonight, anyway."

This from Inspector Combridge about an hour after they had arrived at the house of death.

They had examined the desolate rooms, and talked and theorized and gazed at the sphinx-like silence of the screen, and all the time Professor Blinkwell had stayed beside them, and given them such help or information as he could, and yet all the time with an unspoken, impalpable suggestion that he was ready—waiting for them to go.

He had made a formal offer at the first that he would watch with the Inspector through the night in the fatal room if he really thought that anything could result, and the Inspector had declined—not because he had been up all the previous night, but that he had an appointment at the Yard at 9:30 which he must not miss. Now it was 9:15, and he was evidently ready, if not in haste, to go.

But Evelyn hesitated. She had a curious reluctance to leave that dim and silent laboratory with its secret unrevealed. It was badly lighted, with two gas-jets only, which the Professor, a methodical man, had turned low as they had left it to examine the room on the other side of the landing. Now she looked in at the half-opened door, and saw dimly on the left-hand wall the glimmering whiteness of the screen which held the secret of all this mystery—the secret which it would not yield. Between it and the central table, imagined rather than seen in that shadowy gloom, she knew that there was the dark stain of the life-blood of Wilfrid Ralston, whom she had known with some measure of familiarity, if not intimacy, for the past we months. She imagined him raising himself with difficulty upon his hands, and dragging his broken body through the pool of his own blood toward the table—why? Did he mean to pull its contents on to the floor? Had his objective been the milk from the first, or had its fall been a casual accident of which he had taken advantage later? It could hardly have been that he had aimed to get the milk from the first for the purpose for which he had used it. The Professor had pointed out that his blood would have made a better ink. Had he thought of that at the first he would have had strength to write the message in full.

It was no use regretting that now. But suppose she should concentrate her mind on that imagination of the wounded body reaching toward the cloth—clutching it, and then falling back with the cloth still held, so that it was dragged down with all the litter that was on the table at the time? If she could imagine it with sufficient accuracy, would it not provide the key to which the screen would respond? At least, she could stay and try.

"I don't think I'm coming just yet, Inspector, if you don't mind. For one thing, I don't want to get home till—well, till Lady Barbara's gone to bed. You know you promised you'd do the explaining for me, and you've evidently put that forward into your next day's programme."

"No," the Inspector answered, "I telephoned Lady Barbara after you had left Belleville Gardens, and explained the whole matter. She was very kind about it, and very reasonable—very reasonable indeed. I think, Miss Merivale, she may have already known more than you supposed. She asked particularly about the dog."

"Well, anyway," Evelyn answered, looking as nearly disconcerted by this information as it was her nature to do,

"I don't need to be back early tonight. I arranged with James to let me in up to twelve-thirty—and if it's five minutes later I don't suppose he'll have locked me out. If you don't mind, Inspector, I want a bit of time by myself in that room."

We may suppose that Inspector Combridge hesitated, because there was some delay before he replied, but he was not one to let his indecisions appear. After a long minute he said, "It's really a question of how long Professor Blinkwell is staying, and whether he has any objection. If he's going to use the room for his own experiments…?"

The Professor said, "I may be here for some time. If Miss Merivale wishes to remain in the laboratory, I have some calculations on which I can work in the other room. If she is concerned for the conventions—well"—with a smile—"they've both got locks. But I don't suppose she'll wish to stay very long. It's not a very pleasant room to be in after dark. Not at midnight, anyway."

"It's no use trying to scare me like that, Professor. I never was worried about ghosts, except by the way they won't turn up when they're expected. I've watched for them for hours before now."

"You'll remember," the Inspector added, "there's a telephone in the other room. You can ring up Thornton's Garage, round the corner, for a taxi any time you want to go home. I shouldn't try too long if I were you."

He went down the stairs to the back door, which was still the one in general use, and then turned and called to her something about Lady Barbara, which she could not hear, even when he repeated it. She ran down after that, as the shortest way of hearing what it might be, and followed him to the door.

"Never mind Lady Barbara," he said in a low voice; "here are the keys. You'd better lock the door when I've gone, and keep them till you see me again. And remember the telephone will ring up Hoxton Police Station as well as the garage. I don't think you ought to stay long here. Not after the Professor leaves, anyway. And tell your driver to call at Scotland Yard on the way home. You can let me know then if you've found anything out, and give me back the keys. I shan't leave till I know you're safely on the way home."

He went quickly at that, aware that he was already late for Sir Reginald, if that gentleman had traversed the North Road at the speed which he had proposed to do. Well—she might find something out. A girl of nerves, and a good brain. And there couldn't be much risk with the Professor there.

Evelyn shivered a little as she returned up the echoing uncarpeted stairs, but she did not waver in her purpose to see it through, let the Professor stay or go as he would.

CHAPTER XXVI.

IT was 10:45 P.M. before Sir Reginald Crowe was announced, and by that time Inspector Combridge had spent a very uncomfortable hour, more or less, with Sir Henry, who had resolved to wait and hear for himself what, if anything, the banker might have to say which would alleviate his present anxiety as to the comments which were likely to be made upon the Metropolitan Police organization when the second inquest was held.

His temper was not improved by the information that the Inspector had allowed Miss Merivale to remain in the house which had been the scene of the previous murders. He was in a mood to foresee trouble, and his language was forcible and picturesque as he imagined the public criticism which would follow any further catastrophe.

He suggested the possibility that the Professor might leave Miss Merivale in the empty house, and that her dead body might be found there next morning.

"'How came Mr. Wilfrid Ralston to be alone in the house of murder?'" he suggested, with a clumsy sarcasm that the Press might adopt. "'The police put him there to discover his brother's murderer, which they had failed to accomplish....' 'How came Miss Merivale to be alone at night in the room which had been the scene of the mysterious murder of Mr. Wilfrid Ralston a few days ago?' 'The police took her there to discover the murderer, which they were unable to do.' Nice it'll sound. It's no use you standing there, Combridge, looking like an injured saint. You know it as well as I do. 'They took her there in a fast car.' They'll probably ask whether it was the same one that we used for. Yes, of course you can if you like. It's the only sensible thing to do."

Inspector Combridge, who was not entirely free from anxiety himself, but was one of those who will take a risk coolly if at all, had suggested that they could easily telephone and ascertain that Miss Merivale was safe and well, "and if we don't get a reply, I can have someone round from Hoxton Station in about three minutes."

The connection was made almost at once. "That you, Professor Blinkwell?" the Inspector inquired. "I thought I should just like to know that you are all right, and that...."

"Don't talk to him!" Sir Henry broke in testily. "Tell him to get her to the phone. Tell her straight that she's to go home I Or, rather, tell her she's wanted here at once. I'll talk to the young woman! I'll...." He stopped to listen to the conversation at the instrument. The Professor had been asked to fetch Miss Merivale, and had replied that he had been to her only a few minutes before, and had been badly received. She was sitting watching the screen from the farther side of the room, and said she was not to be disturbed. But he would have another look, and if he didn't ring up again they would know that she was all right.

"That won't do, Combridge. You must stop that nonsense at once. Rung off, has he? Then get him again. What's that? Crowe coming up? Very well. I don't suppose it'll take five minutes to hear what he's got to say. Not at this time of night. We'll just finish with him, and then ring up again, and if she won't clear out of that house you'd better fetch her yourself."

Sir Reginald came briskly into the room, with nothing of the appearance of a man who, like the Inspector, had not made the acquaintance of a bed during the previous night. Sir Henry Clobson, who had taken his usual eight and a quarter hours' sleep, was the only one of the three whose outwardly ruffled aspect indicated the mental ordeal through which he was passing.

"I'm sorry," Sir Reginald began, "that I'm not on time. It's snowing up North, and to come through as we did— well, it's the first time and the last for me. It's all right for you to tell me you'll bear me out, Inspector, and you'll have to be as good as your word. There are three or four reports with the number of my car on them being handed in now. But you couldn't be much use to us if we'd killed a child, as I thought we had, coming through Leicester. Nor to the child either. As it is, there's nothing worse than a dog with a broken leg that I've had to bring on in the car, as the owner wasn't in sight. But when I think that it might have saved that man's life if I'd let you know what you asked at the first—I don't say that it would, and I don't say I was wrong, whether or not—but, all the same, I didn't mean that any more time should be wasted before I got at the facts, if you were right, or could tell you to look elsewhere."

"I suppose, Sir Reginald, you've found out something of importance, or you'd scarcely have made an appointment with me at this hour," Sir Henry interposed. He felt, among other things, that the conversation should be addressed rather less to the Inspector, and more to himself. Sir Reginald Crowe looked at him for the first time since he had shaken hands as he entered. He was no respecter of persons, a fact which had had its influence both upon the successes and failures of his adventurous career. "If I hadn't found out something of importance I shouldn't be here myself at this hour. It's your job, not mine," he said curtly. "I want you to tell your men to get me Sir Joshua Isaacs on the phone. Tell them not to be put off. I know he won't be at home. They've got to find out where he is, and get him to come to the phone himself. Yes, I mean the Chairman of Barham's Bank, of course. There's no one else of that name. They'd better say that I want to speak to him on a matter of great urgency. He's more likely to come to the phone for me than for you. I don't mean to be rude when I say that, but he knows that I know his rule that he won't do business at night, and that I shouldn't ring him up if there wasn't need."

Inspector Combridge did not wait for the formality of Sir Henry's consent to this procedure. He was already at the telephone, giving the necessary instructions. "We ought to have him in a few minutes," he said with confidence.

"Then I'd better tell you how matters stand while we're waiting for the call to come through.

"I had that lady's account sent to me to look over, and it told me nothing at all, except that she had a great deal more to spend than a woman needs, and that it went freely enough to the Bond Street shops, and—well, for all the usual foolery that such a woman does buy, when she's never learnt what money's worth.

"I'll admit that but for this second murder coming just when it did I might have turned you down, and said you were wasting time on false scent, but I didn't mean to have any risk that if there were a third it should be my fault, and it crossed my mind to wonder what she did with that £500, and I found that she'd paid it—or, at least, just that amount—into her account the same day that she cashed the cheque at East Grinstead, and, of course, after that, I knew there was something I didn't know, and I meant to find out what it was."

"I don't quite see what you mean," Sir Henry interposed, with more honesty than discretion. "Surely her own account was the most natural place into which the money should go."

"Yes," Sir Reginald answered dryly, "so it was. But why didn't she pay the cheque straight into her account when she offered it to the cashier at her own bank? She went to the trouble of going to East Grinstead—a journey of about twenty miles from where she lives—and bringing the money back to her own bank, where she might have paid the cheque in at first.

"Of course, there was one obvious possibility. Many women get money from men that they wouldn't either of them wish anyone to be able to trace, and men pay money to them in ways that are meant to secure that result. But our manager didn't think she was that sort, and the circumstances were a bit odd, even for that. It would have been more natural that he should have drawn the money, and given it to her in cash, than that he should have expected her to go such a distance to cash the cheque for herself. So in half an hour after that I had all the resources of our bank turned on to that woman, and I dare say that even you don't quite know what that means.

"It took about two hours to get me the vital link—that Miss Myra Porchester wasn't Miss Porchester at all. She has three other names for banking accounts of different kinds, and very interesting they were, and when I found that she was really the niece of—but I mustn't tell you that yet.

"Well, to cut it short, we went on tracing moneys from one account to another, and it got more interesting all the time. It was evident that a lot of money was going about that didn't show any clear origin in the way of trade, and the amounts grew and accumulated, and sooner or later they gravitated toward the account of a firm of stockbrokers in Pontefract.

"When I learnt that much I didn't lose any time. There are things that are better said than written, and I went where I could find out. The stockbrokers' account was at Barham's Bank, not ours, and I saw the manager there, and when I'd put my own cards on the table, and he knew who I was, he gave me all the help that he could, and we weren't long in finding out that most of this money finds its way in the end to the credit of—oh, well, that of the uncle of Miss Myra— Myra being her real name, though the other isn't.

"The only stipulation he made was that I shouldn't give away the names of their customers without the consent of Sir Joshua Isaacs himself, and I agreed to that, because it was only right, and when you know who it is...."

The telephone bell rang, and Inspector Combridge took the call. "Sir Joshua," he explained, as he laid down the receiver, "was at a reception at Dalton House. He said that he wouldn't talk business there for all the crowned heads in Europe, with the presidents thrown in, but he expects to be home in about half an hour, and if Sir Reginald likes to ring him up personally there...."

"Damn the fools!" Sir Reginald exclaimed irritably. "They should have put him through. That didn't mean anything. He always talks like that. You might tell them to try him again."

But when the next call was put through to Dalton House the reply was that Sir Joshua had just left.

CHAPTER XXVII.

EVELYN turned up the two ancient gas-jets. She turned the first one out, under the impression that she must have been turning it the wrong way when so little happened, and she had to light it again. Their combined efforts did no more than dimly to indicate the recesses of the gloomy room. The screen glimmered in a ghostly way with a surface which was not as of glass, but of a faintly milky opaqueness.

She sat down on the dusty floor, changing her position several times to get a view of the room as closely alike as possible to that which the screen would receive, and yet to be so placed that she would be able to transfer her glance to its surface when she wished to do so.

But she soon realized that this was an impossible thing. The reflections which the screen would give her, from any angles, would be different from what she could see from the same spots. Her best course, she decided, would be to sit immediately beneath it, and then to turn round, trying to keep the imagination in her mind as she gazed into the surface which held the truth, which it was so shy to show.

The room was still in the disorder in which it had been found when Professor Blinkwell and Sergeant Middleditch from the Hoxton Station had discovered Wilfrid Ralston's body; only, the body was gone, and there was nothing left to show what had been, except the stain of the dark pool

155

on the floor and the long smudge where he had dragged himself to the table.

Evelyn moved opposite to the screen, and for some time she gazed directly into it, trying by force of will to reach the secret of its shadowy depths, Time after time she thought that something was taking shape within it: time after time it eluded her, even as she thought herself to be on the point of triumph. Giving this up at last, and turning to her previous purpose, she sat beneath the mirror, and tried to visualize Wilfrid Ralston as consciousness came back to his eyes, and a bewildered, terrified realization that he was an injured and dying man. Clearly and more clearly it seemed that she could see him thus, as his eyes steadied to the purpose that he had formed, and he raised himself on his hands, and drew himself with gasps of pain, toward the table which was his goal. And as he did this she knew that the blood broke again from his back where the bullet had entered. Did it spurt upward in a red fountain of jets as his heart beat, or did it only soak into his clothes, and drip from his sides as he struggled along the floor? She must shirk nothing, imagining it as it had really been, if she were to succeed in the object on which her mind was set.

After a time she tried transferring her glance to the mirror, and withdrew it, baffled by a blankness which seemed indifferent to any imagination or effort of will that she could bring into operation against it. And then she was suddenly disconcerted by a thought which should have come to her at the first. Even if she should succeed, she would see nothing of a value to repay her effort. She would only regain the scene from the point that she was endeavouring to reconstruct. She would see nothing of the murder, and the murderer would have gone. To gain that which she sought she must reconstruct it from a much earlier point; and how could she hope to do that, knowing nothing of what had happened, or who had been in the room?

As she thought thus, and was of more than half a mind to abandon an enterprise that seemed so hopeless, she was so still in the quiet room that a mouse came out from its farthest corner, bread that lay among the confusion of the dirty floor.

As she looked at it idly she was aware of a slight noise at the door. It was so slight that she was unsure whether it were imagination only, but—had not a key turned in the lock? Very slowly, very cautiously, very quietly indeed, was it not being withdrawn? She made a sudden motion, as though to rise, and then restrained herself—if it were true that she were being locked into the room, she might only hasten whatever trouble it foretold if she were to show that she had discovered the position in which she was placed. Frightened and doubtful, she became still again, but the impulsive movement had been sufficient to startle the intruder, and it had run back to the skirting from which it came.

From the landing without, loud in the stillness, there came the sharp creak of a board. What evil thing was without in this house of death? For a moment she sat very still, almost too frightened to move. Had the Professor left? Did he sit at his calculations in the closed room on the other side of the landing, unaware of the sinister shadows that moved between him and her? She felt that they might be contriving her death, as they had contrived the deaths of two others already, while she sat idly watching a mouse. *Watching a*—in a flash she had guessed it. *Watch the mouse* was the message that Wilfrid Ralston had sought to send them from the pit of death into which he had fallen before the words were completed.

It was so easy to understand when once it were guessed that she blamed herself that she had not thought of it before. It was just the kind of idea that would come readily to the subtle ingenuity of Wilfrid Ralston's mind. Doubtless he had seen the mouse come out from its hole as he had sat working silently, and so the idea had come. It would be useless to promise the Inspector that he would show him anything that might be done in the night unless he could establish some starting-point from which it would be taken up on the screen.

And so—the seemingly careless scatter of crumbs that were still unmoved—crumbs that would draw it back to the same place, so that there would be at least an approximate similarity in its movements. Perhaps there had been some further subtlety by which he had planned to secure a more exact duplication of movement, but that was beyond guessing now. She could be thankful that the floor had been left with the floor unswept, and resolved to put her fears aside, and to wait in silence till the mouse should gather courage to come forth again.

She must keep still—keep still—forget the landing and the fear without. That must wait, to what end it would. She could only pray that she should be undisturbed till the secret should be in her hands.

The mouse came out for a few inches, and then paused. In the stillness she heard the telephone bell ring in the room across the landing. The sound gave her the confidence of recalling that Inspector Combridge would be waiting at Scotland Yard till she should call on her way home. Who would have been likely to have locked her door? It was a nervous imagination, a woman's weakness, such as is the jest of men. Did she not hear the Professor's voice at the instrument, or was that imagination also?

She had not moved at all, but the mouse must have heard the bell. It had gone back a few inches, but after what seemed to her an endless pause it came on again. Now it was feeding among the crumbs. Its movements one night must be very like its movements another. When she moved it would run back. Ought she to watch it do that? Was it an essential thing, or would it spoil the experiment entirely? If it ran back any moment while she watched, might it not be spoiled in the same way? If she had got that which was needed, every moment was an added risk. She decided that the best way was to rise quickly, and turn as she did so to face the screen while the vision of the mouse making its little movements among the crumbs was still retained on the eye's retina. Should that fail there would be no more hope, for tonight at least. She rose with the thought, and faced the screen.

There was no interval, no pause of blankness, no struggle of will to overcome the enigma of the shadowy screen. Clearly and instantly she saw the mouse that was eating among the crumbs. The milky opaqueness of the screen was gone. The whole surface was become a reflection of the dimly lighted room, but not as it was tonight. She saw the face of Wilfrid Ralston, as he sat opposite the screen at the farther side of the table. He was manipulating some plastic substance between his hands. Now he looked up, and it seemed that their eyes met for a moment, and then he was looking toward the other side of the room, beyond the range of her vision in the position in which she stood. Step by step she moved backward, afraid, if she should turn her eyes aside, that the vision would fade away. She knew where she was standing now. It was on the dark stain of the dead man's blood—the man who sat there, so lifelike and so near, unconscious of his approaching doom.

She gazed into the screen with a bloodless face. A watcher, had there been any, might have thought that she herself was the ghost, looking down on the living man. But she did not faint nor falter in the purpose which possessed her mind. Only—she could not stand thus for—how long? She had not thought till now that the vision in the screen would move no faster than had the event itself. If the mouse had come out several hours before the time of the murder, for that space of time she must watch the process of that room of death. She felt backward around the table till she found a chair. She was sitting now in the same position as that in which Wilfrid Ralston sat on the screen. In the same chair....

She could see now that the Professor was near the door. He had his hat on, and a long cloak. Evidently he was ready to go. When he had gone it might be that there would not be long to wait. She could not hear the words, but she could tell that they were both talking about the screen. She could tell that from their gestures, and from the direction of their eyes. Wilfrid Ralston had put down the dough-like substance he was kneading. He was rubbing it from his hands. He got up and walked round the table toward the screen. She looked back at the Professor, and as she did so he drew his right hand from the pocket of his coat, and she saw the pistol that it held.

"*Wilfrid!*" she cried, in a voice that rang through the empty house. "*Wilfrid, look!*" But there was a streak of light across the dimness of the visioned room, and Wilfrid was on the floor.

Self-control came back to her with a realization of her own peril. "How," she said aloud, in a quiet and steady voice, "how shall I get out of this?"

Had he heard when she screamed—the Professor still working quietly, as she supposed, in the other room? That foolish, foolish scream! Would he dare to harm her, the Inspector knowing that they had been left together? Could he dare to let her go free? Should he guess what she had seen?

If it had been fancy that her door was locked, might she not walk quietly down the stairs, and let herself out unseen? It was no use waiting here.

She crossed the room, and going quietly to the door she turned the handle, but the lock held. It had been as she thought. Then she remembered the bunch of keys that the Inspector had given h7er, and, still moving very quietly, she got them out of her bag. It was fortunate that the Professor had not left his own key in the lock. Probably, like hers, it was one of a bunch.

She saw that the fact that he had locked her into the room, thinking that he had her safe till his own time—for what?—might be the thing which would save her. He could not have guessed that she had the keys.

Quietly as the lock had been turned before, so it was turned again. Very quietly, not knowing what she might see, she looked out on the landing.

It was all vacant and still. But there were sounds from the other room, the door of which was open a few inches, throwing a band of light across the landing, and on the banisters of the back stairs. The sounds puzzled her, as did a current of cold air that came from the slightly opened door, suggesting that a window was lifted in that farther room. What could be the meaning of that?

Still very quietly, and with a courage more commendable than her discretion, she crossed the landing and looked in.

She saw first that two boards had been taken up, and that a number of aluminium boxes (or so she thought them) had been lifted out of the cavity. If the Inspector's theory were correct, Dudley's hidden cache had been found. She saw that the Professor stood at the open window, and was hauling in a loose rope. Evidently the boxes were being lowered to someone in the yard of the long-empty premises that Messrs Shard and Nesbitt were unable to lease or sell.

She had the sense to see that the sooner she could get clear away the better it was likely to be for her; and as the Professor came from the window for another box she turned toward the stairs, and, loud in the silence, a board—perhaps the one she had heard when the Professor locked her in—creaked beneath her feet.

In three strides the Professor had gained the door. She saw the pistol in his lifted hand. She had the sense and the courage not to attempt a useless flight.

He did not ask her how she had got out. He was not a man of useless words. The keys were still in her hand.

He said, in an easy, conversational voice, which contrasted with the quickness of his approach and the menace of the lifted gun, "You mustn't go yet, Miss Merivale; you'd better go back now. We'll have a talk later. I'll take charge of the keys."

"I'm afraid I can't wait," she answered, in a voice that shook just a little, try as she might. "It's later already than I meant to stay."

"I'm afraid you must," he answered, quite pleasantly. "You should have thought of such possibilities before you pushed yourself into matters which would have been much better left. I'm busy for a few minutes longer, and we must have a talk before you go, but I don't intend to be late myself."

"You have no right to detain me at all," she answered, with all the courage she had. After all, she had the keys. She was at the stair-head. She doubted that he would attempt violence. As to shooting—would it not be to make his own fate certain, the Inspector knowing that they had been left together?

"Miss Merivale," he said quietly, "don't make any mistake. I can't afford to let you go like this. If you go back and wait for a few minutes in the next room till we have time to talk, you'll be no worse off than you are now. If you take another step toward those stairs, I shall send a bullet through your neck, which, I tell you frankly, I shall be sorry to do."

"You'd be more than sorry," she said steadily, feeling surprised at her own coolness. (Did people always feel like this, with that small black muzzle before their eyes?) "It's a thing that you'd never dare. Inspector Combridge would guess who'd done it at once."

"On the contrary, Miss Merivale. I'm about the last that anyone will suspect. You'll see that if you think. I leave you in the house, as you've insisted on being left, and I go home. Tomorrow morning you're found shot. That was how it was with Wilfrid Ralston. Anyone would see that I should never dare to establish such a coincidence as that. It would be too flagrant to be believed. And that isn't all. There would have been three murders, not two. And it would be the easiest thing on earth to prove that I'd nothing to do with the first. I was fifty miles away, more or less, at the time. It's a tale that no jury would believe. And, anyway, it's my risk. You won't be alive to see what happens. I shan't warn you again."

"Very well," she said, as casually as she could, "as you're so pressing, and if it doesn't mean that I can't be back at 12:30. I don't want to be locked out."

He made no answer, but walked back with her to the room she had left, taking the keys, as he did so, from a reluctant hand. He looked with some embarrassment at the shuttered window. "I shall require your word," he began, and then, "No, you'd better come with me." He led the way back to the other room.

"May I telephone Inspector Combridge, to tell him I shan't be long?" she asked, rather fatuously. "I needn't mention anything else."

Perhaps he disliked the reminder of the Inspector's name. Perhaps the feminine absurdity of the suggestion annoyed his mathematical mind. From whatever cause, he answered with an irritation which he had not shown previously.

"No. There's only one thing you can do, and that's to sit still. It'll be over all the quicker for you."

Evelyn did not like the last words, and she liked a slightly satiric tone in which they were spoken still less.

She must take what comfort she could from the fact that she was still alive, and that if the Professor had meant to shoot her he could have done so without all this bother.

But he might think it best to do that at the last minute before he left. He was a careful and methodical man. One, she felt, who would avoid any needless risk.

If he shot her, and were then disturbed before leaving, she would be rather awkward to explain. On the other hand, after all she had seen, she would be very awkward alive under such circumstances. Very awkward indeed. She wished that this aspect of the matter were less evident than it was.

Suddenly she was aware of a tigerish hatred for the Professor, such as she had never felt for anyone in her life before. It was a feeling of which she had not known herself to be capable. A desire to spring, to fight, to do *something* to make sure that he should not kill her, and then go free. She did not mind so much if she died, if she could be sure of her revenge. She looked round in vain for some weapon that she could reach from where she sat before he could intervene.

She could see nothing, and was conscious that his attention was quietly upon her, even while he went on lowering the remaining boxes to his unseen helper below. "I shouldn't do anything foolish, Miss Merivale. It's far better to have a talk."

Better, she thought, for whom? Better for him, perhaps; but for her? She could not see how any talk would result in a position by which he could afford to let her go free. And she was just playing his game sitting there. Doing what he wished. Might it not be better, or at least no worse, for her, if she should force the position now? And yet—time might be on her side. It might bring some rescue, some relief. The Inspector would get anxious when she did not arrive. She wondered that he had not telephoned again before now. Could she reach the instrument, if he did, with a quick leap, and call out something that would make the Professor's fate sure, even though she were shot as the words were said? It must be getting very late. Probably after midnight now. She looked down at her wristlet watch. It was 10:47—and her watch was two minutes fast.

"Oh, no, we shan't be late," the Professor remarked, with a recovered pleasantry. (Was there anything that he didn't see?) "I've promised not to be late home tonight. I shouldn't have been here at all, only that these boxes had to be cleared, and no one else could come in without being noticed, the police watching River Street as they do. I expect there's a couple of them there now."

"It's been an unfortunate business," he went on, as though thinking aloud, as he drew the rope in for the last time, and closed the window down, "an unfortunate business from end to end. It wasn't on my advice. It's a lesson they won't forget for a good while to come, to leave those on the spot to decide. I've said before now that it's always a mistake to keep your method and change your man. He might have lain there for a month, if it had been properly done.... And now, Miss Merivale, I want that formula."

"Can I go, if I give you that?"

"Not just yet. But you certainly won't unless you do. It's a case of one thing at a time."

"I don't see what use it'll be to you, unless—" She paused, conscious of the doubtful discretion of what she was about to say.

"No? Well, I haven't asked you to see anything, have I? The trouble with you has been that you see too much."

She looked through her bag, delaying every second that she could. Surely *something* would intervene! As she handed the paper for which he asked, she wondered, should she tell him that it was a useless thing? Or should she keep still, and if he shot her after he thought that he had obtained everything from her that would be her revenge, that the secret would be lost to him, without the possibility of recovery—lost through the act of his own hand? She only doubted whether it would be revenge enough.

"Do you swear that this is correct, Miss Merivale?"

"It is the original paper," she answered. "Just as I had it from Mr. Ralston. It is in his handwriting."

He looked at it, and appeared satisfied. But he would have no doubt. He told her the oath that she must swear, and she repeated the words, not listening to what she said.

"And now, Miss Merivale," he said, in a voice of curter decision, "you will please step on to the landing."

She knew it then beyond doubt. He would shoot her as she stood at the head of the stairs. She could not see why he should want her there. She supposed it to be part of some scheme to make it appear that she had died in a certain way. Perhaps he would leave the boards up, and it would be made to appear that she had surprised some burglarious work during the night. No one, she thought, would suspect him in such connection as that. And the unfastened window would show how the house had been entered from the grounds of the empty factory.

"Professor Blinkwell," she said, "you can take your hand out of your pocket. The formula would be dear at a shilling."

CHAPTER XXVIII.

"I DON'T wish to risk obstructing your call, Sir Reginald," Inspector Combridge remarked, "but I should like to get on to Bell Street again when I can; I'm not over-easy about the way things are left there."

"Surely, Inspector," the banker answered, "you're not leaving anything to chance there? I should have thought you'd have had it watched day and night, so that a rat couldn't go out or in without having its pedigree taken."

"It's not that, Sir Reginald. They're watching the place well enough. They're doing that from the Hoxton Station. It's someone who's inside now who's on my mind. I left Miss Merivale there an hour or so ago—"

"Not Lord Britleigh's sister?"

"Yes, Miss Merivale. I understand that she knows you, Sir Reginald."

"Did she say that?" Sir Reginald Crowe was one of the least likely of men to be communicative about his personal affairs or feelings, but his curiosity was aroused by the remark, as the Inspector may have intended that it should be. They were sitting there waiting for a call that did not come, and he was, perhaps, inclined to something less than his normal reticence, which is a common effect of the omission of a night's sleep. He rose to the bait, though not eagerly. "Did she say that?"

"She implied that she had done. In fact, she seemed more than usually interested."

"If Britleigh hadn't been such a fool, trying to force the pace, I should have married that girl," Sir Reginald exclaimed abruptly, on an impulse that he regretted even as the words were said.

"She is not too old now," the Inspector suggested, but met with no inclination to' continue the conversation on those lines.

"What is she doing in River Street?"

The Inspector explained. It was a detailed explanation, and took some time. It was made longer by occasional questions from Sir Reginald, seemingly designed to prolong it. He certainly took an interest in Evelyn Merivale. At the end he said. "Well, I don't think I'd have left her there, Inspector, if I'd been you. Not without a couple of constables at the door. Not but what she'd be right enough. I never met a girl better able to look after herself. Not that I really met her at all. I saw her at the theatre once or twice, but I don't know that she saw me. And then I went down to Saxton, and in the morning she wasn't there. But when you say you've left her there alone you don't mean it literally, do you?"

"Not exactly. Of course, the house is being watched from both streets. And there's one of Vantons' directors on the spot too. I told her not to stay after he left, and to drive round here when she came away, so that we shall know she's all right. I'm rather hoping she'll have something to tell us that'll be worth hearing."

"Which director was it?" Sir Reginald asked. "Not Britleigh, I suppose! There'll be a cat-and-dog fight going on in that house by now, if it is."

"No. It's Professor Blinkwell—"

"WHAT!" Sir Reginald sprang up with the word. "He's the—" He stopped himself abruptly, remembering the word he had given, and reached over for the telephone, but it was already in the Inspector's hands.

"You needn't say any more, Sir Reginald. You've made it quite dear. Is that you, Fordyce? See that my car's at the door. There's not a second to lose. Ring up Hoxton. They're to surround the Bell Street place, and not let any-one through, either out or in. *Anyone*, tell them. If neces-sary, they're to shoot to kill. Men, not women, of course. If it all looks quiet, they're to lie low till I get there. That'll be in about ten minutes from now. Yes. If there's any row going on, they're to break in. But not if it's quiet. But no one's to leave. *No one*." He hung up the receiver.

"Look here, Inspector," Sir Reginald burst out, with a display of agitation that seemed somewhat beyond the oc-casion, "I don't think that's right. They ought to break in at once. There shouldn't be a second lost. You don't know what—"

"No," said the Inspector, "but I soon shall. I haven't lost a second, except the last we that I've been listening to you. We shall be there in ten minutes. But till then, if the place is quiet, Miss Merivale must take her chance. This is a bigger thing than a woman's life. I'm not going to have the Hoxton men muddle it up before I get on the spot. I know Middleditch too well."

"But look here, Combridge," Sir Henry exploded.

"I think Sir Reginald's right. I won't have—"

"I'll report to you in the morning, sir. I'm sure you'll excuse me now." The Inspector was gone with the word, and Sir Reginald at his heels.

Sir Henry Clobson decided to ring up Hoxton at once, and then became undecided again as he reflected that he would make himself responsible to his subordinate (he didn't think of it quite in those words) if anything went wrong as the result of his interference. It was far better to be in a position to blame Combridge under such circum-stances, and to be able to rely upon his resources to get them out of the mess.

CHAPTER XXIX.

THE Professor regarded Miss Merivale for some moments in a thoughtful silence.

"There seems to be a little difficulty here—a mutual difficulty. Perhaps we had better sit down, and talk it over. I must mention again that my time is short, as I have made a promise not to be late home tonight, but I should appreciate any suggestion that you have to offer."

Evelyn answered boldly, though she was still conscious of the rapid beating of her heart, as it had leapt at the sudden peril from which a ready word had—for the moment—saved her: "Professor Blinkwell, I may be wrong, but I believe you meant to murder me as I went out of that door."

"Not exactly," the Professor answered, with his usual precision, "but very shortly afterwards."

"And I just wanted you to know that it would be a silly thing to do, because, among a lot of unpleasant consequences, you'd have lost the formula forever."

"You mean that the one you have given me—"

"Is just what I had from Mr. Ralston, but it needs someone to understand it. Someone alive. You seem to have a habit of shooting the only people who know how that invention can be made to work."

"There is no need to insist on that point, Miss Merivale. I have admitted that I am in a difficulty, and I

170

have invited suggestions from you. I suppose you don't like the idea of being shot?"

"It mightn't be so bad for me as it would be for you afterwards."

"I'm glad you look at it so reasonably. As a matter of fact, anyone who is shot—efficiently shot, that is—in any vital part is exceptionally fortunate in these days of deaths which are so skilfully delayed and protracted. Except the domestic animals, that are slaughtered for food— But if I wander like this, I shall be late after all. You are mistaken, Miss Merivale, in your main contention. I do not apprehend any disconcerting consequences to myself, whether you go free or not. It is a question of account entirely. If you go free and give such information as you think will be most damaging to me, it may involve a substantial reduction in my present income. If I carry out the programme which I had planned, I shall save myself from loss, but you tell me—whether truly or not—that the formula will be finally lost. You are an efficient liar, as most women are, but I am disposed to believe you in this instance. I tell you frankly that I dislike both the alternatives, and I invite any suggestion you have to offer, always remembering that it must not keep me here."

Evelyn was still playing for time. She said, "I see the difficulty as well as you do, but it is not so easy to see the way out. Even if you promise or try to frighten me into telling you how the formula can be worked, you won't know that I've told you the truth, and if I promise to say nothing about what's happened tonight, you can't be sure that I shall keep my word."

"That is a good deal of the truth," the Professor admitted, "though not all. That you would be truthful about the formula is a very unlikely thing, for though I can observe you to be a young woman of a pleasant pulchritude, it does not disguise the fact that you are, at this moment, of a very venomous disposition. I have to take into account that you are of a lower moral standard than myself, and would do me harm, if you could, even though it might be of no benefit to yourself—a course of conduct of which I am so radically incapable that it is only by scientific deduction that I can recognize it to exist at all."

He was silent for a moment, and then continued, "Miss Merivale, I will tell you frankly that if you could give me that formula, and offer some convincing proof that you had done so, I would let you go free, as the price of that information, rather than it should be lost, as is otherwise a too probable thing. My difficulty is that I cannot see how such a proof can be given."

"I can also see a difficulty," she answered, "but it is of an opposite kind. If I could convince you that I had given you the formula correctly, how should I be sure that you would not alter your mind, and murder me after all?"

"It is a risk, Miss Merivale, which I am afraid you will have to take."

"It is a risk which I shall most certainly decline."

"Then I must ask you to be good enough to walk to the head of the stairs, as I originally proposed."

"Then you must think I'm a fool."

"Not at all, Miss Merivale. You have nothing to lose, and a good deal to gain, by so doing.... You would still be able to walk for the short distance that I require, after I had shot you in several very painful ways, which I should be sorry to have to do. As a sensible girl—"

"Professor Blinkwell," Evelyn said desperately, "suppose we both give each other our words not to say anything about tonight, and we meet here again tomorrow, when we've both had time to think it over. Of course, I don't want to get shot, and of course you don't want the formula to be lost. I don't suppose you want to shoot me either, if you can see another way out."

"But that, Miss Merivale, is just where you are wrong. I regret to say that I am conscious of an atavistic instinct, which I observe rather than approve. It would give me a pleasure of an unusual kind to see you walking toward the head of the stairs with the consciousness that you were just about to be shot through the neck, and subsequently to watch you die. It is an animal instinct which I should control without difficulty under normal circumstances, but it will be a subordinate satisfaction that I am able to gratify it, though the loss of the formula is too high a price for any excitement that I can experience in that way.

"I invite you, for the last time, to give me the true interpretation of that formula, and I assure you that, if you do so, I will let you go free without exacting a promise which you would not keep. The consequence of your interference would be a substantial loss of income to myself, as I have already admitted, but nothing more serious than that, though I can understand that you may think differently—and against that I shall be content to place the value of the formula that you have surrendered."

"If I could trust you—" She hesitated.

"You haven't much choice."

A policeman's whistle shrilled from the direction of the empty factory. The next moment there was the sound of a shot—and then another.

"It seems," the Professor said, "that there's no time to lose, or I shall be home late after all. Quickly now, if you please, Miss Merivale. It's the formula, or the stairs."

But Evelyn looked back at him with defiant eyes, her courage rising with the knowledge that there was help—at the worst, there would be vengeance—at hand. She made no motion to speak or rise.

The Professor saw that he wasted time while he delayed to argue in a different way. He raised his pistol, and fired. She was seated in an armchair of an ancient pattern, with a horsehair seat. Her left hand had been on the rail, and she withdrew it sharply as the wood splintered. She looked down on a hand from which the top joint of the little finger had been shot away, so that it hung by a mere shred of flesh and skin.

"Unless you want another—" he began.

She thought of the darkness of the landing—of her conviction that, for some reason, he did not mean to fire till she was near the head of the stairs. If she could throw herself down a second earlier. If she could roll down the stairs. It would be easy for him to miss in the dark.

She rose meekly, and walked from the room.

CHAPTER XXX.

IT is disconcerting, when the resolution for heroic action is taken, to find that, by some impish gesture of Fate, the scene upon which we enter has been changed to a comedy, or has been adjourned for an indefinite period.

Evelyn walked from the room at a steady pace, every sense alert, and listening for the motions of the man that followed, or rather—and that was the unexpected complication—of the man who didn't.

She was as certain as though she had turned to look that he was still seated as he had been when he fired the shot which had smashed her finger—the finger which was now becoming horribly painful, and which she was holding in its place with the handkerchief in the other hand, from which the blood dripped as she walked.

Unless he were waiting to follow her when she had had a leisured opportunity of assuming her required station, or unless he were capable of firing a bullet which would turn the corner of the door at an angle of about seventy degrees, it appeared that he must have abandoned the intention which, Evelyn was sure, he had meant quite seriously but a few seconds ago. Anyway, she abandoned hers. However great might be the peril in which she stood, she was not going to risk making herself a laughing-stock for the rest of her life by rolling down the stairs when there was no pressing necessity for that undignified progression. Besides, her finger— What might have been ignored at the issue of life or death became a convincing argument as she paused alone in the half-darkness of the landing. For pause she did, when it might have seemed the obvious thing to run for the stairs in these seconds of unexpected respite. But she was puzzled at the strangeness of the event. Either it had been all a bluff, or his courage had failed at the last, or—was it a trap? Did she walk to some cunningly contrived death at the stair-head? Ideas of trap-doors and rotating boards—of Amy Robsarts and Sweeney Todds—rose vaguely to vex her mind. Anyway, she hadn't the keys. She would be a fool to walk down the stairs, and then stand helpless at a locked door.

The only sensible thing to do was to walk boldly back, and tell him to stop being a fool, and give her the Inspector's keys. She'd got to get out somehow, and have something done to her hand, the pain of which became more severe as the urgency of other emotions weakened. Such were the thoughts of ten seconds' space, as her steps slackened on the bare landing boards, and she turned back somewhat irresolutely to the door she had left.

"I shouldn't go back there, Miss Merivale," said a voice from the opposite darkness. A man's voice—the words being advice, the tone an order. The voice of a man who was accustomed to give orders in the assurance that they would be obeyed. Evelyn stood where she was.

"On the contrary, Miss Merivale," came the Professor's voice from the opened door, "if you will be good enough to come back, I shall be pleased to surrender my pistol to your—remaining hand." (It was evident that whatever reverse of Fate had overtaken the Professor had not disturbed his characteristic precision of mind and speech.) "It is in every way best that I should be unarmed while interviewing the gentleman of the intermittently projecting shadow."

Evelyn hesitated but for a second between these contradictory orders. She was almost certain that she knew the voice that came out of the darkness, though, if she were right, she had only heard it twice previously. It was that of her brother's friend, Reggie Crowe. If he thought that he could order her about like that— She walked back into the room from which she had come, and listened to the Professor's explicit and (for him) almost urgent instructions as to how she should take charge of his loaded weapon.

"You'd better take this, Reggie," she said to the man who was now beside her.

"As I haven't one of my own," he remarked easily, "perhaps I had."

"I suppose you'll say you saved my life, after this," Evelyn remarked, with some natural bitterness. The feelings of a young woman who is under that obligation to a man she dislikes have never been properly exploited in contemporary fiction.

"No, I won't mention it," Sir Reginald assured her kindly.

"I'm not sure that you did," she added, with an admirable honesty. "You may have saved me from something a good deal worse." That undignified idea of the stairs! (Suppose—under the mistaken idea that the Professor had been behind her—with Reggie looking on—)

"Yes?" he said, in some bewilderment. He could not quite see—"

It isn't a matter I can discuss," she replied coldly, regretting already that she had given such an opening for further questioning. Sir Reginald was still somewhat puzzled, but if she wished him to think, or to think herself, that he had saved her from worse than death (an expression which frequenters of picture-palaces will understand very readily) he saw no reason why he should endeavour to remove so satisfactory an idea.

"If the gentleman had not overlooked that his shadow—" the Professor began.

"I was in some difficulty, being unarmed, and it occurred to me that it might have that effect."

For the first time the Professor looked really cross.

"You needn't put your hands up," the official voice of Inspector Combridge intervened, as he came into the room, with a little crowd of dark blue uniforms in his rear. "They'll do very well as they are." The handcuffs clicked.

"I am sorry to appear in any way to object to this somewhat melodramatic performance," the Professor said quietly, gazing down at the ornaments on his wrists, "but I have promised not to be late home tonight."

He looked upon the Inspector with an air of mild disapproval, as upon one who had failed to live up to the expectations that he had raised. "Inspector Combridge," he said, "I thought you had more sense."

"Professor Blinkwell," the Inspector replied, without any appearance of being impressed by this reproach, "I am arresting you for various offences in connection with the possession and sale of prohibited drugs. You will be formally charged in the morning with these and other offences, and probably with complicity in the murders of Dudley and Wilfrid Ralston, and I have to warn you that—"

"He shot Wilfrid himself." The interruption from Miss Merivale, now reseated in the horsehair chair with the splintered arm, and mainly conscious of the pain in her injured finger, and a determination not to faint among this crowd of policemen.

"You know that?"

"I've seen him do it."

"Then I charge you with the murder of Wilfrid Ralston.... Miss Merivale, what is wrong with your hand?"

"I've got the top of the little finger nearly shot off. I don't want to move the handkerchief I'm holding it on."

A police-surgeon came forward from the little crowd that filled the background of the room. "You'd better let me see it," he said. "Come into the next room. We'll have a look, and see what can be done."

She hesitated for a moment, feeling a premonition of pain that would be worse than anything she was enduring now, if he should "have a look." She did not feel that she could stand much more. But Sir Reginald Crowe was helping her to rise, and she was not going to be foolish.

"All right, Reggie," she said, "I'll come."

"How did it happen, Miss Merivale?" the Inspector asked. He had his duty to do, and held a straight course through the contending emotions around him.

It was the Professor who answered. "It represents the result of the lowest form of argument, Inspector. That which is on the physical plane. I am sorry that I should have had such frequent occasion to descend to your level." He indicated the handcuffs that were round his wrists.

"I shall charge you further with the unlawful wounding of Miss Merivale."

The voice of Sir Henry Clobson rose on the landing. The dark blue group parted respectfully as the Assistant Commissioner entered the room.

"I couldn't go home, Combridge," he said, with a fussy importance contrasting with the cool efficiency of his subordinate, "till I knew how you had got on. I see you've got the scoundrel. Is the young lady safe? Have you got any evidence?" He looked round the room, and with curiosity at the lifted boards.

"We caught two men in the empty warehouse next door. One of them's shot in the leg, and I'm sorry to say that Sergeant Middleditch is rather badly hurt. He did very well indeed. We owe that capture to him. And we've taken some cases; but, of course, we haven't examined them yet." He wished Sir Henry had had the sense to go home. The last thing he wanted was to discuss such matters in that crowded room. He was hoping every second to hear that the van had arrived, and that he could remove his prisoner. See him safe in a cell, and get a few hours' sleep for himself, and he would know what to do to make the best of this.

The voice of the Professor interrupted his thoughts.

"I believe," he was saying, "that you are Sir Henry Clobson. If so, I suppose that you have authority to relieve the atmosphere of this overcrowded room, and if you will be good enough to do so, we can begin to talk with intelligence."

Sir Henry answered somewhat explosively. The insolence of— Then he met the Inspector's eye, and bent to the will of the stronger man. The Inspector was already giving the necessary instructions. In half a minute the room was clear except for himself, Sir Henry, the handcuffed man, and Sir Reginald Crowe, who had silently re-entered.

CHAPTER XXXI.

"IT OCCURRED to me that I might explain matters to better advantage (to your better advantage, Sir Henry; I don't credit you with sufficient altruism to be concerned about mine) when you had removed your retainers, which I am glad to see that the Inspector has had the good sense to do."

"If you desire to make a statement—" Sir Henry began.

The Professor stared upon him in a frank amazement. "I'm not quite such a fool as that," he said, with a curter intonation in his normal mildness. From that moment he ceased to notice Sir Henry, and addressed himself exclusively to the Inspector.

"If you are not prepared to adopt Sir Henry's suggestion," the Inspector remarked, "I'm afraid I may have made a mistake."

"I think you will be quite satisfied that you haven't before you've done. I may be able to tell you one or two things worth hearing. Anyway, you can ask. If they're not too important, I'm quite willing to tell you freely. If they're too valuable for that, we must just talk over the price."

Inspector Combridge saw very dearly the nature of the negotiation on which they were entering, but he reflected hopefully that he might have a shock for the Professor, who could have no idea of the extent of the information with which Sir Reginald Crowe was proposing to furnish him. If he were calculating to escape by the betrayal of his English associates....

He opened with a question which did not advance beyond the outposts of the position that he was resolved to storm.

"I don't think you've got any idea," he said confidently, "of how much we already know. But there's one point that puzzles me, and I don't mind admitting it. Why did you send Elijah Ringbolt away just before Dudley Ralston was done in?"

The Professor did not take any exception to the implications of this question, nor did he attempt to bargain for the information.

"The man you call Ringbolt, who was better known to me as Beery Joe—though whether that name was given in consequence of a tendency to resort to alcoholic refreshment at short intervals, or on account of a fancied resemblance to a popular film star, I am unable to say—was employed to watch Dudley Ralston, to observe how he could best obtain access to the house if it should become desirable, to report if any goods were removed from the premises, and to be ready to silence him promptly if it should become necessary to do so.

"He somewhat overacted his part, and attracted the notice of the police, so that it became a matter of routine discretion to send him away.

"The man who was subsequently employed was a sailor of Eastern origin. In the somewhat excessive way in which he killed Dudley I have no doubt you have observed that the head had been almost severed by a blade which must have been extremely sharp, and of a shape which is of a more general popularity in Eastern than in Western lands. The only error was made—"

"We call murder something worse than an error in this country!" Sir Henry exploded. The cool way in which the fellow sat there, and—

"We misunderstand each other," the Professor went on calmly, without looking at the Assistant Commissioner. "I did not mean that the killing of Dudley Ralston was an error. It was a necessary thing. The mistake, for which I was not personally responsible, was in instructing two quite different agents in the same manner.

"The man you call Ringbolt had been told that if at any time he should receive instructions to silence Dudley, he should inflict such injuries to his head as would be sufficient to prevent his survival, and then throw him down the front stairs. As his brother seldom, if ever, went into that part of the house, the deceased would have remained undiscovered for an uncertain but sufficient time, and his death would have been attributed to a fall down the stairs in the dark.

"Beery Joe would have carried out this order with exactness, but the excessive ferocity or zeal of the Lascar who was subsequently employed led to the quite needless effusion of blood which prematurely disclosed the incident, and removed the possibility of the adoption of the otherwise most natural explanation."

"You had better give us the name of that murderous," Sir Henry broke out again.

"I think not," the Professor answered, still addressing himself to Inspector Combridge. "The man has been paid, and the incident closed, so far as he is concerned. The information would only be used to make further trouble. Is Sir Henry entirely destitute of any compassionate feelings? The man must have his own. He may have a waiting wife."

"But you admit," said the Inspector, "that you shot Wilfrid Ralston with your own hand?"

"I was not aware that I had done so. Miss Merivale's enterprise has robbed that statement of any novelty which it might otherwise have possessed."

"If we're going to discuss what Miss Merivale's done, perhaps she'd better come in," Sir Reginald suggested.

"If she's quite fit," the Inspector answered without enthusiasm. His interest in the young lady may have been less than that of the one from whom the suggestion came, and he preferred to manage this conversation in his own way.

"I should think she'd be fit by now. I left her in the other room. She said she'd like to rest for a few minutes. I expect she'll be glad to come here now. It's not a very pleasant place to be in." He went out with the word, and returned with her. She was very pale, but by no means of a dispirited aspect. The work of the police-surgeon had been swift and skilful. The use of a local anaesthetic had not prevented the stitching of the nearly severed joint being a very painful ordeal, but it was over now, and everything seemed to be coming out very well. Very well indeed. Even Reggie wouldn't be so bad if he quite understood that—

"But for Miss Merivale's ingenuity," the Professor was saying, "in discovering the meaning of that unfinished scrawl, which I may say that I have—"

The Professor's remark was not destined to be concluded, for Sir Henry broke in again with his usual impetuosity.

"Yes. That reminds me, Combridge. That was one thing I came to tell you. Withers has been all through the 'm's in the *Oxford Dictionary*, and two of the others have been over different ones at the same time. I had the report just as I was coming away. They say it's an awful letter. Most of the words wouldn't mean anything. 'Missionary,' and 'Mahatma,' and 'mangel-wurzel.' If it had been 'b' or 'c'—"

("I suppose he means that Crowe's better than Merivale," Sir Reginald remarked in an audible whisper to his nearest companion. "No, don't try to move away like that. You're not fit. Jolly rude of him to make such a suggestion. That's what I was trying to say.")

"But they are unanimous that what he intended to write was either 'man-trap' or 'man-hole,' and they are strongly inclined toward the latter word, because there is a man-hole in River Street, from which it is evident that an armed gang could emerge quite easily."

"Unless," Sir Reginald suggested gravely, "they have failed to give due consideration to the claims of monkeys, or marigolds of the more exuberant varieties."

He was not one who was accustomed to jest at Assistant Commissioners in unseemly moments, but a shadowy smile on a girl's lips at his earlier remark had raised his spirits to a momentary irresponsibility.

Sir Henry considered these surprising suggestions with a puzzled seriousness, and a pause which might have ended discordantly was broken by Evelyn's remark, "It sounds a very good guess, Sir Henry, but the word really was 'mouse'." In a few words she described her experiences of the earlier night. As she finished the Professor looked at the little group of his captors with amused eyes. "Going to use that evidence?"

"No," the Inspector answered. "I don't think we shall." He thought that there would be plenty without that.

"Neither do I," the Professor answered confidently. "Inspector Combridge, it's time to come to the point. I don't want to be here all night, and I'm sure you don't. What would it be worth to clear up the international drug traffic once for all?"

The Inspector knew what it would be. It would be the biggest thing in his career. The biggest thing ever done at Scotland Yard. If all this trouble would lead to *that*, it meant that he would be something more than a chief detective-inspector in six months' time. Or less.

He answered coldly, "It might be worth a free pardon to the man who would give such evidence as would secure that result."

"But a case of murder—" Sir Henry interrupted.

"I don't think we have any evidence of murder, Sir Henry. Not legal evidence. We couldn't use what Miss Merivale saw on the screen, and in a few days, as I understand, if not less, the picture will have faded away." If Sir Henry would only be quiet! He didn't *want* any evidence of murder, if he could lead it to this.

"Do I understand, Professor Blinkwell, that you are prepared to offer such evidence?"

"Certainly not," said the Professor. "I am not going to have my reputation ruined over this incident." His voice even rose slightly as he contemplated such a possibility. "Have you considered that it might involve my resignation from the Board of Vantons, and perhaps other difficulties in retaining control where my investments are placed?"

"That might be better than Dartmoor."

"Inspector, if you would only cultivate a habit of logical thought, you would be a very able man. Why should you assume that I cannot give you the required assistance without personally involving myself in the resultant publicity? Can you wire to Shanghai in code? Can you control the line so that the message will be sure to arrive at the very end of the day? You will pardon these questions. I do not wish to teach you your work, but you will remember that you are dealing with much cleverer men than yourself—or the Assistant Commissioner. Then, if you will have these handcuffs removed, I will give you an interesting address. Thanks."

He wrote a name and address on a slip of paper and passed it over the table.

"But this," said the Inspector, "is the address of...." Words failed him as he gazed at the Professor in an astonishment that was not entirely free from an angry suspicion that he was the subject of an inopportune jest.

"Yes. What did you expect? Not the expected, surely? You're not such a fool as that. Wire them to arrest *everyone* there, and search the place. During the night. Tell them to arrest everyone, and make it plain that there'll be some vacancies if they try to think for themselves and let someone go whom it couldn't be, and you'll get all that you want."

The Inspector thought quickly. If this were a hoax, and such arrests were made without reason, there would be at least one vacancy to be filled, but it wouldn't be at Shanghai. The Professor followed his thought very easily. He said, "Do you trust Crowe? I'm not going to have you coming to my office. Apart from other reasons, it might give the alarm. And I'm not going to be in danger afterwards, if you let some of them slip through the net, as you probably will. If Sir Reginald will come to my office tomorrow afternoon, I'll give him all the documentary evidence you require, with the names of three or four that you can approach as witnesses after you have made the arrests. After, not before. Well, gentlemen, I think that's all. I told you that I mustn't be late tonight."

He rose, and was making for the door, when Sir Henry Clobson interposed angrily. "Wait a moment, my man; you're not getting off like that. We'll hold you by the heels till we've—"

Professor Blinkwell looked at the Inspector with a restrained exasperation. "Will you explain?"

"I'm afraid, sir, we shall have to let him go now. If his arrest were to get about before...."

The telephone bell rang as he spoke.

"That will be for me," the Professor said with assurance. He picked up the receiver. "Yes, Myra. I've been a bit longer than I intended, but I'm coming now. I dare say, Inspector, you'll detail one of your men to pass me out. By the way, Miss Merivale, you'd better have this formula back. It's no use to me."

But the fate of Wilfrid Ralston's invention is another story.

ABOUT THE AUTHOR

SYDNEY FOWLER WRIGHT (1874-1965) penned over seventy volumes of science fiction, fantasy, classic mysteries, historical novels, poetry, and non-fiction, many of them being published by the Borgo Press Imprint of Wildside Press.

www.ingramcontent.com/pod-product-compliance
Lightning Source LLC
Chambersburg PA
CBHW032010240626
47153CB00003B/1198